My TRUE

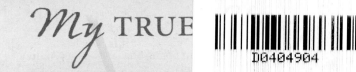

Hero
at
Dunkirk

Vince Cross

■ SCHOLASTIC

For the Read family, Graham Spain, Sheila Johnson, Audrey
Carter, Sandra King and all those who remember Joe with
affection and admiration...

Scholastic Children's Books
Euston House, 24 Eversholt Street,
London, NW1 1DB, UK
A division of Scholastic Ltd
London ~ New York ~ Toronto ~ Sydney ~ Auckland
Mexico City ~ New Delhi ~ Hong Kong

Published in the UK by Scholastic Ltd, 2010

ISBN 978 1407 11783 6

Printed and bound by CPI Bookmarque, Croydon CR0 4TD

2 4 6 8 10 9 7 5 3 1

Author's Note

What makes someone a hero? Is it something they're born with, like being tall or good at maths? Or is it something which happens to them by accident – by being in the right place at the right time?

There were thousands of acts of individual courage during the Second World War, but few fifteen-year-olds among the heroes. Hundreds of ordinary people put their lives at risk during the rescue of British and French forces from the beaches of Dunkirk in Operation Dynamo at the end of May 1940, but Joe Read was the youngest. What they achieved between them changed the direction of the Second World War, and prevented a national disaster. The Britain we live in today might not exist if it hadn't been for them.

Joe's is a largely unknown story. It attracted some newspaper interest in the weeks afterwards, and on anniversaries of the evacuation people have occasionally remembered him and his father Wally. There may have been a brief television feature about them in the 1960s, twenty-five years after the events. Of course, Joe's own family have never forgotten the story, and this book is dedicated to them. Today, in an age of instant celebrity, it would all have been very different but back then Joe received no official recognition, and he went on to live an ordinary and at times very difficult life. He died relatively early at the age of 57.

No one now remembers a great deal about the young Joe. So what follows is an imaginative re-telling of how he came to be a hero. I've tried to stay true to Joe and Wally Read's own words about what happened at Dunkirk, and to what family members could tell me about their wartime home life in Camden Square. I've made up some of the rest of the story, and if you look in the historical note at the end of the book, I say a bit more about that. I hope nothing I've written about Joe, his family, his friends and his home town gives offence to anyone: I've grown to have enormous respect for Joe and Wally's bravery and the seafaring traditions of Ramsgate.

Vince Cross

PART 1

DRIFTING

Friday 10 May 1940: 4.45 a.m.

These days Joe Read always slept with his bedroom curtains open. He liked the way the first faint glimmers of light woke him each morning. He reached for his torch, checked the time on his watch under the sheets, then slid out of bed and into his clothes. A few years ago he'd still have been secretly afraid of the shadows in the house at Camden Square, but with the announcement of the 'black-out', darkness was something you just had to cope with. Mind you, you needed to be careful picking your way along the streets in the pitch black, otherwise you might walk slap bang into a lamp-post. It was no laughing matter. Old Fred Sumner had done that very thing on his way back from the pub last week, and now he had a broken nose for his trouble.

'*These* days'. Strange days! Things weren't turning out for Joe the way he'd imagined. Not one bit. When he'd left Ramsgate's Holy Trinity school last July, rising fifteen and feeling for the first time as if he was a proper man and really belonged in his long trousers, he'd been so looking forward to the spring of 1940. At last he'd be free to work with Wally, his dad, under the golden sun every day. Together, the two of them and Bill Matthews, they'd clean up the *New Britannic* for the new season, and then each morning and afternoon they'd take the punters out of the harbour and round the Brake lightship to the Goodwin Sands, or just down the coast to Deal. One hundred and twenty passengers. Three bob a time. Three trips minimum a day, depending on the tides. A hundred quid cleared on a really good day, if you included tips and the takings from the bar. A fortune, and in cash too! His dad and Bill would tell tall tales of wrecks and storms, the holidaymakers would *ooh* and *aah* and occasionally be sick (hopefully over the side and not on the deck) and Joe could tinker with the *New Britannic's* engines and coil ropes to his heart's content. It had been his dream for years – to be free of stuffy old school, take his place among the other boatmen on Ramsgate's harbour front, and become part of its history...

And not just the harbour's history – his *family's* history. The Reads had been the heart and soul of Ramsgate's seafaring for at least three generations and probably more than that. But now that nasty, evil little bloke Hitler had spoiled it all. Since war had been declared with Germany last September, Ramsgate had changed so you wouldn't know it, and in no way for the better. This year there'd be no holiday-makers, no trips out to the Goodwins, no tall tales except in the bar of *The Queen's Head* during the increasingly jittery evenings. And, without the cash the tourists brought with them to Kent's sunshine coast, there wouldn't be money to pay for Wally's beer either. Or anything else come to that. What were they going to do? Joe knew Wally and Flo were worried. He'd heard them talking in low voices when they thought he wasn't listening. And as if that wasn't enough, the war had taken his brother Ernie away in the cruellest of circumstances. Now Ernie was on a Merchant Navy ship who knows where. Joe's nightmare was that they'd get a message one day to say he'd been sunk and taken prisoner by Jerry. Or worse.

Joe unhooked the precious binoculars from the back of the chair and looped them around his neck. He tiptoed over number 38's creaking floorboards, past Wally and Flo's bedroom, and down the coal-black shaft of the stairs to the kitchen. The key turned smoothly in the front door's well-oiled lock and then Joe was leaping up the steps which led onto Camden Square. It took two minutes through the chilly morning air to reach the gardens in front of the handsome Georgian terrace where Alderman Kempe, the Mayor, could look out over the Channel from his office windows. After that it was no more than another two or three hundred paces down the hill and across an open space past the Pavilion to the pier. The long stone bulwark stretched along the east side of the harbour before it turned at ninety degrees to form the jaws of the haven's mouth.

The harbour was crammed full of boats, fishing smacks, privately owned yachts, pleasure craft (including the *New*

Britannic) and now a growing contingent of naval boats too, but it was so early that there was almost no one about. What was the point in any owner of a smack getting up before dawn these days? Where was any Ramsgate boat going to go now for pleasure or profit? True, fishing out of Ramsgate didn't compare with thirty years ago anyway, when the shoals of herring could still be easily found, and fishermen came with their trawl nets from all over England and Scotland to ply their trade. But this year, with German U-boats lurking in the waters of the Channel, and the constant danger of floating mines which could blow you to kingdom come, no more than a quarter of the remaining fishing boats were venturing out, even when they were allowed.

'*Allowed*', because the Navy were taking over Ramsgate, and my goodness weren't they full of what you could and couldn't do! There were hundreds, maybe thousands of sailors in town. To be fair, they were there for a reason. Who could say what the Germans might get up to next? They'd already made short work of the Poles and the Czechs. There wasn't much to stop them rolling through the flat lands of Belgium and Holland, and just about the whole of the British army had been sent to northern France to try to prevent them doing the same to the French. So the Royal Navy had spread itself out along the Channel coast to guard the southern approaches to England from invasion, and Ramsgate was one of the natural places for them to be. Almost overnight

7

the centre of town had turned into one big naval base. It even had a name – *H.M.S. Fervent* – and perhaps strangest of all, the *Merrie England* amusement park had become the Navy's control centre.

Out on the pier one or two fishermen were patiently stalking a sea-bass breakfast with rod and line; a couple nodded at Joe as he passed. Wasn't Wally Read's son growing up to be a fine lad! '*Must be as tall as his dad now. What do you reckon? Five foot nine, and broad with it! Don't he look the spitten image of his mum though, God rest her soul. Can't you just see Daisy in the boy's face?*'

Joe raised the binoculars to his eyes. The dawn had come up quickly and now it was clear enough that he could see the far side of the Channel. He could make out a long smudge of yellow sandy beach and to its right, shimmering in the haze, the buildings and smoke of a town, probably Dunkirk. More interestingly, perhaps two thirds of the way to the French coast there was a line of grey British warships, glittering in the early morning sun, heading east. But just then, before he'd properly had time to take in the scene, a sudden roar of aircraft engines made him jerk his head around. A flight of four Hawker Hurricanes, line abreast, were sweeping in low and fast over the cliffs from the direction of Camden Square. They passed just a few hundred feet above the harbour before climbing out into the skies over the Channel. The fishermen tutted and moaned about their peace being shattered. It'd all be the fault of those RAF toffs if they went home empty-handed this morning. Joe watched the planes as far as he could, but even in the near cloudless skies, they soon became dots too small to follow. Leaning his elbows on the pier rail he turned his glasses back to the ships and the sparkling sea.

"See any U-boats, Nelson?" a voice said softly.

Joe jumped. A beanpole lad an inch or two taller than him was suddenly standing beside him. Maybe Joe had been distracted by the planes, but he hadn't seen or heard him coming. The newcomer's deep blue eyes were twinkly and teasing. The accent was unfamiliar. He was aged maybe nineteen or twenty and he was dressed in a scruffy Navy uniform. His trousers barely had creases. His shoes had seen better days.

"Well, I wouldn't be likely to, would I, mate?" Joe answered scornfully. "Since they'd be grubbing along the bottom. Don't need to be in no senior service to work that out."

"Fair enough," the other lad answered smoothly. He was getting used to Ramsgate's prickliness when it came to naval uniforms. "So what *is* so interesting out there then?"

Joe took another look. One of the ships – a cruiser, judging by its size – seemed to be taking avoiding action, veering hard to port away from the rest of the battle group. But what was it avoiding? As Joe watched, smoke belched from the for'ard guns of the ship immediately to its west, once and then a second time. The wisps of smoke hung in the air, as they would from a lit cigarette. Another of the ships, last but one in the convoy, seemed to be listing hard to port, and unless Joe was mistaken, smoke hung around it too, though not from its guns. Was it on fire?

"Well, funny you should ask, but I dunno … not really…"

"Let's have a look then…"

Joe was caught unawares. He was half-way to handing over the glasses when his hand touched the brass plate on their side and remembering, he hesitated.

"I won't drop 'em, I promise. Or run off, if that's what you're thinking…" said the other lad. He sounded offended at the thought. "Go on, give 'em over!"

Reluctantly, Joe gave him the glasses.

The boy from the Navy took them up, adjusted the focus, swept the horizon with a seasoned eye, adjusted a second time, and then looked again.

"An exercise," he said dismissively. "Just practising. In case. Goes on all the time. Nothing out of the ordinary. Not these days."

He spoke quickly, too smoothly, so Joe wasn't really inclined to believe what he said. These Forces types, with all their secretive 'Careless talk costs lives' stuff. They pretended to know it all. As Wally said, if they wanted to know something about the waters round Ramsgate, why didn't they just come and ask the people who'd spent their whole lives out there. They knew the secrets – the tides, the shifting

10

sands, the winds.

As the stranger lowered the binoculars his fingers felt the raised brass plate on their side. He turned them over to look. He read what was written there: *'To Thomas Read, in recognition of his gallantry at sea. With the grateful thanks of the people of the United States of America. Thomas Woodrow Wilson, President. 1919.'*

"Fancy glasses," he said, returning them to Joe, "Where did they come from?", thinking: *'Junk shop, most like...'*

"My great-uncle, Tom Read," Joe answered, relieved to have them back in his hands again. "He got 'em for pulling American sailors off the wreck of a ship called the *Piave*. Old Tom was on the lifeboats for 49 years. We buried him last year, but my uncle – he's called Tom too – he said I could borrow them for the weekend if I was careful. He's on the lifeboat now an'all ... the new one ... not the one that saved the *Piave*, of course. That was the *Charles and Susanna Stephens*. The new one's called the *Prudential*. Young Tom's the assistant mechanic, and these days he gets paid a wage for it. The old boat was a sail-ship, but the *Prudential*'s got a Weyburn petrol engine. You can crank ten knots out of it with a following wind, Tom reckons. Might have been alright when they built it in 1926, but these days they need something with a bit more poke, I reckon..."

The words poured out in a torrent of pride for his family and passion for the sea. It made the other lad's heart go out

11

to him. Maybe southerners weren't all as stuck up as his dad had made out. Maybe it was only the Brylcreem Boy footballers at Arsenal and Charlton.

"Well, I know a fair bit about you then," he said. "So I suppose I ought to introduce myself. My name's Stan Wainwright. From Manchester."

He offered Joe his hand.

"And I'm Joe Read," said Joe, shaking it.

"So all your people have got salt water running through their veins, have they?"

"This is Ramsgate, ain't it?" said Joe. "What else would you do with yourself? Everyone's born with one foot in the water round here. Unless you want to do up a boarding house and spend your time tidying up after trippers. My dad's the gaffer of the *New Britannic*. If it wasn't for the flippin' war and the fact we can't move in the harbour for your lot, I'd get him to take you out for a blow round the Goodwins."

"That'd have been fun," said Stan, and meant it.

"Too bad," Joe replied. "The *Britannic*'s going nowhere for now. My old man reckons your mates'll have their maulers on her before the month's out."

Stan thought that was probably right. He knew what he'd read up in the office at *H.M.S. Fervent*. The Navy had its eyes on 'borrowing' as many pleasure craft as it could, to patrol the coast and help keep the Channel clear of enemy mines so that it was safe for merchant and naval shipping to pass. Many of the mines were magnetic, and so were a menace to any ship with a metal hull, which meant the big ones carrying cargo, or the ones that belonged to the Navy. Once they homed in on your underside, it was one big 'Kerboom' and that was your chips. The *New Britannic* was likely made of wood, so the mines wouldn't be a danger to her. Not the magnetic ones any road. The Navy wanted boats like the *Britannic* to go fishing for high explosives. That was what the country needed, but it would be tough on their owners.

"Where d'you live then, Joe?" Stan asked.

"Up there. Camden Square," said Joe, pointing.

"One of those fancy houses up on the front? They're real posh, they are."

"Nah. What d'you think? Like we're royalty or something? We're behind them lot. At the back of Queen Street."

Queen Street was one of Ramsgate's main shopping streets.

"Still … pretty nice though…" Stan sounded wistful – a bit homesick.

"Search me. Depends what you're used to, I suppose. It's just where we live, ain't it! Handy for the harbour. Handy for the town centre. We had one of your people in our spare room, till he got posted last week. He seemed to think it was all right."

Wheels were starting to turn in Stan's head. He was billeted with a Mrs Arkley, who lived on the distant west side of town and was a sour old biddy. She looked at Stan as if he was the scum of the earth, and pretended not to understand a word he said because of his accent. The house was so dingy and dirty Stan got out each day as fast as he could for fear of catching something. He was itching for the chance to move out permanently. The people in charge of billeting arrangements occupied the next office to Stan at *Fervent*, and only the previous evening he'd been bending their ears with a view to a change of scene ASAP.

"I don't suppose by any chance that room's still free, is it?" he asked Joe.

"Far as I know…" said Joe. "But it's my stepmum Flo you'd need to ask…"

Tuesday 14 May 1940

Flo and Stan shook hands on the deal that weekend, and soon after he came off duty at *Fervent* on Sunday evening, Stan arrived on Number 38's doorstep with his kit bag slung over his shoulder, ready to move into the Reads' back bedroom.

"The lad looks all right," Flo had said to Wally. "Bit of a charmer, if you ask me…"

Wally harrumphed. "That's what you said about the other bloke…"

"Well, maybe I did," she answered, "And he weren't too bad in the end, was he, Wal? Kept himself to himself. Left the room clean when he went."

"He was Navy. Same as this one. What more do you need to know? Messing up the harbour with their petty rules and regulations and who goes there and keep yer shoes polished. I don't want it at home an'all."

"The Navy allowance ain't much, but it'll come in handy," said Flo. "You said yourself how we'll be on short commons, and there won't be no B&B this year. So be nice to him, Wal. If you can…"

Joe worshipped the ground his dad stood on, and usually

15

if Wally said a thing Joe would say the same to someone else the next day. But even he thought his dad had a bit of a down on the Navy. It wasn't their fault they'd been put in Ramsgate. He liked the idea of having Stan around. It'd be different. Stan said daft things which made him laugh.

"Knock, knock," had been his first words to Joe on Monday morning.

"Who's there, then?"

"Tank."

"Tank who?"

"You're welcome I'm sure…"

At Tuesday evening tea-time they were all around the table downstairs – bread, margarine and potted shrimps. The wireless was on and the six o'clock news was just about finished. There wasn't much to cheer you up, unless you were German. Bad things were probably happening on the Belgian border. Jerry had invaded, and the Belgians weren't putting up too much of a fight, reading between the lines. And in England the Secretary of State for War, Sir Anthony Eden, had announced the forming of a group called the Local Defence Volunteers for men over 18 who hadn't been called up to the Armed Forces.

"Suppose you'll be putting your name down for that, Wal?" asked Flo. Wally didn't know whether she was serious or not. He grunted.

"Marchin' up and down and playin' around with guns

16

ain't what I want to do. But I'll tell you something for nothing. I'll kill any Hun I find on our beaches with my bare hands."

But it was very nearly the last thing on the bulletin which really made them sit up and take notice.

"And now a message from the Admiralty for all owners of small pleasure craft..." said the plummy-voiced newsreader. "The Admiralty has made an order requesting all owners of self-propelled pleasure craft between thirty and a hundred feet in length to send particulars to the Admiralty within fourteen days of today if they've not already been offered or requisitioned... And finally ... the news headlines again..."

As Joe knew only too well, the *New Britannic* was fifty-four foot long. It was self-propelled, with six-cylinder and four-cylinder Ford engines. It hadn't already been offered to the government or requisitioned. Wally and Joe had hoped against hope that it wouldn't come to this, though in the past few weeks they and the other boatmen had often talked about the possibility as they'd hung around on the quayside, hands in pockets. Now Wally stood up and turned the wireless off with a snap of the wrist that threatened to break the switch. He sat down again heavily. He took his cap off, and ran his hands through his hair, right hand, left hand, right hand, left hand.

"Well that's it then. Your lot are finally doing for us," he said bitterly, spitting the comment across the table as if Stan was personally responsible for what had been said. "That's the *Britannic* gone and we'll never see her again."

Most of the time Wally was a lovely bloke – everyone thought so. He might not say much, but he'd help out anyone in trouble. But sometimes he had moments of bleakness and black despair. Stan knew enough not to argue, and Joe … well, Joe had always found his dad's moods horribly painful. After Joe's mum Daisy's death, Wally had sometimes been like it for days on end. At first Joe had tried to offer some comfort, but the words never seemed to come out right. And now the thought of losing the *New Britannic* was as painful to him as it was to Wally.

"Maybe it'll just be for a while, Dad. Then we can have her back. Maybe the war'll be over in a few months."

"You're talking out of your rear end, son…"

"Wal!" said Flo, genuinely shocked. "You shouldn't speak to the boy like that…"

"He hears a lot worse on the boats. He's got to know, and you've got to know, this bloke Hitler'll take a lot of beating. Ain't that right, Stan?"

Stan was surprised to find himself asked for an opinion.

"Well, the Navy needs all the help it can get, Mr Read. I know mine clearance is a concern…"

But Wally wasn't really listening. "God, what a lousy year…" He stood up again, hesitated, and then moved to the door, putting his cap back on. "I've had enough, I can tell you. I'll see you later, but don't wait up."

Joe went to follow. Flo put a hand on his arm.

"Let him go, sweetheart," she said as the door slammed. "He'll be all right in an hour or so. Let him have a good moan at everyone down at the pub."

It *had* been a lousy year. Just when Joe had thought things might be getting better, all the bad memories had been re-ignited. 1938 had been OK. Wally had finally got round to marrying Flo. And a month or so earlier, although perhaps only to get back at her new stepmum, Joe's sister Nora had married her beloved William. Nora and Flo were chalk and cheese and were never going to hit it off. England had nearly beaten Australia at cricket, despite Don Bradman, and Len Hutton had scored more runs than anyone else ever in a single innings. Even Wally, who considered all sport a waste of time, thought that was OK. Then came 1939, and the slow realization that war with Germany couldn't be avoided. And everyone knew what a new war might mean. They'd had a taste of it twenty-five years earlier when the Germans had sent air-ships to drop bombs on London. But modern aeroplanes meant that Germany was now only a couple of hours away. The Dorniers and Junkers planes could fly much, much faster than the Zeppelins and could drop far more and heavier bombs. Thousands would die in a nightmare of explosions and fire. So worried had Mayor Kempe been that he'd told the borough surveyor to draw up plans for tunnelling into the chalk cliffs of Ramsgate so that the population would be safe if the air raids came. Now there were shelters for sixty thousand people, double the number who actually lived there, under a sweeping semi-circle of roads around the northern half of the town. Nowhere in England was better protected. But still ... how much warning would they get? Would there be time to run?

And then not long before war was finally declared in September 1939, Old Tom had died. The funeral had been almost as splendid as the one for Joe's grandfather five years earlier. All the great and good of the town, as well as all the harbour folk, had turned up on a grey late summer's day to pay their respects to a man who had helped to rescue over 500 people from the seas around Ramsgate over nearly fifty years. Imagine! Tom had first enrolled as a lifeboatman in 1886, when Queen Victoria still had nearly fifteen years of her reign to go, and he'd only retired as coxswain in 1935. If the RNLI rules had allowed it, Tom would have celebrated fifty years of marriage and fifty years in the lifeboat all within a month. Even then he was only sixty-eight when he died – "No age!" Flo had said. And then she'd caught Joe's eye, and they'd both filled up, as they remembered that Joe's mum had been just 47 when the cancer had taken her.

Even after that, death hadn't done with the Reads. Joe's brother Ernie had married a sweet girl called Ivy, and at the back end of 1939, they'd had a baby boy. But Ivy had always been a bit sickly, and what started as a cough turned into something much worse as Christmas 1939 passed into the New Year of 1940. By February Ivy was dead too – from tuberculosis. "I didn't know you could go like that … so quick," said Ernie, in disbelief. He took compassionate leave from the Merchant Navy for a few weeks, and spoke very little to anyone all that time. Then he packed his bag and went back to his ship and the baby went up the road to Ivy's parents. "Blood's thicker than water", they'd said, though Flo would have loved to have had a child of her own to look after. As she said, they weren't exactly short of space.

"Knock, knock," said Stan, getting up from table.

"Who's there?" answered Joe without much enthusiasm.

"John…"

"John who?"

"John the Navy. I've got to go back to work. If you want to chew the fat I'll be around tomorrow evening."

Joe looked puzzled. Why would he want 'to chew the fat'? It wasn't an idea that made any sense. Men *did* things: they didn't need to gossip like women.

Wednesday 15 May 1940

"So can I see this boat of yours?" Stan asked after tea. He'd spent a long day stuck in an airless, pokey office, and now he wanted some fresh air.

"Sure, whenever you want," said Joe. American films played every week at the Picture House, and sometimes Flo took Joe along for company. He liked the way Americans talked. He looked across at Wally, who was on his way to *The Queen's Head*, to check that was OK.

"You go ahead, mate," his dad replied. "Just don't sail her all the way to Calais."

"Dad took the *Britannic* across the Channel once," said Joe as he and Stan walked down to the harbour. "But they never let him in the port. He don't like the French much." He smiled. "A bit less than he likes the Navy, and that's a fact!"

They stepped inside the boat, and Stan ran his hand over the smooth grainy wood.

"Pitch pine," he said. "Whoever built her put some care into that. She's a lovely thing."

"Twenty-three tons," Joe said proudly. "Built by Maynard's up the Thames in Chiswick. Brilliant engines. I'd fire 'em up so you could hear, but it wouldn't do. Fuel's scarce."

"Not much cover if the weather turns bad…"

"One day we'll have a proper wheel-house to keep us dry, Dad says. And maybe an awning for the punters."

Stan's eye fell on the Turk's head knot on the wheel.

"Fancy ropework," he said. "Who did that?"

"Me," Joe said shyly. "I like all that stuff."

"Fantastic," exclaimed Stan. "They tried to teach us in college, but I was hopeless. Couldn't tie a sheepshank to save my life."

"So how come you've ended up sailing a desk?" Joe asked. "Didn't you want to be on a proper ship?"

"Me, I love boats, and everything about the sea," Stan laughed. "Been mad about it since I were a kid. I'm just not… very good at it. Apart from anything else I get seasick as soon as I'm on open water, and nothing seems to cure it. Whereas I'm brilliant at bean-counting."

Joe looked puzzled.

"Bean-counting … paperwork! And right now the Navy needs bean-counters as much as it needs sailors. So … here I am, the best Supply Assistant in His Majesty's armed services. Sorting out the world from inside *H.M.S. Fervent*. Well, someone's got to do it."

They wandered back up the pier.

"What's it like … at *Fervent*?"

"Thinking of joining up? I wouldn't if I were you.

Fervent's a madhouse, like most of the Navy. You think it's all going to be super-organized and efficient. Actually, the right hand never knows what the left's doing. Mind you, what do you expect when you're working somewhere that used to be an amusement park complete with its own zoo? It's not exactly purpose-built, is it! Here, you'd better not let on I'm saying all this. They'll have me up on a charge."

Joe laughed. "Your secret's safe with me. I remember the zoo from when I was a kid. What have they done with the cages?"

"Stripped 'em out, and put in as many huts for ratings to stay in as they could. One lot of monkeys swapped for another. There's folk coming and going all the time." Stan gestured around the harbour. "You can see ... we've got all sorts in here at the moment ... drifters, trawlers, fast motor boats, armed boarding vessels, guard ships, contraband control. You name it, if it can squeeze through your harbour entrance, we've got it, to save Dover getting clogged up."

"What's contraband control?" Joe asked innocently.

Stan looked at him hard. "Seriously," he said. "We're mates you and I now, right? Because you're a civvy, and I'm not, and I could get into trouble for telling you stuff…"

Joe nodded, pleased at the thought of being taken into Stan's confidence.

"OK then, well contraband just means smuggling. One thing we're doing is stopping Hitler getting things that help

Jerry in the war – like fuel or metal. We check shipping passing through the Channel to make sure they're not carrying anything to German ports. And then there's mine clearance work, and checking for U-boats. And watching for spies."

"Spies?"

"Well, stands to reason, doesn't it? If Hitler's thinking about invading, he'll want to know what we've got and where. The top brass think there could be hundreds of spies in England already."

By now they were climbing the hill away from the harbour back towards Camden Square. It was eight o'clock, and the light was just beginning to go.

"There are some caves at the back of *Fervent*, aren't there?"

"Yeah," said Stan. "Our own personal air-raid shelters if it gets rough."

"Talking of smuggling then, let me show you something…" said Joe.

They walked a half-mile or so along the Regency Parade, and onto Victoria Road past the posh front of the Granville Hotel towards the East Cliff. Turning up a side street, they came to the back of a dilapidated house. Joe put his finger to his lips, and climbed a rickety gate into the overgrown garden, beckoning Stan to follow. Stan looked doubtful, but went anyway, on the grounds that he felt responsible and didn't want Joe getting into mischief on his own. Once inside, the garden was in so much of a tangle that you couldn't see the house. A little way inside the gate a metal grille covered the entrance to a shaft. Joe pulled the grille aside and took a torch from his pocket.

"It's only an old bloke who lives here now, and he don't know what's in his back yard," he whispered. "Come and take a butcher's!"

Steps led down into a passage running down at an angle, broad and high enough for one person to walk easily. The walls showed dirty-white in the torchlight, and the floor was greasily smooth. After about fifty yards the passage opened out into a chamber. Joe shone the torch around the walls. The light picked up the shape of a grotesque face carved into the chalk here, some initials there, the date, 1857, visible higher up the wall.

"Smugglers' cave," said Joe. "It leads down to the cliffs. You can reach the entrance with a ladder if you know where. And it's not the only one. We use them sometimes."

"What for?" asked Stan.

"Oh, you know, storing stuff," Joe answered vaguely. He tapped his nose. "Fallen off the back of a lorry ... or a boat."

He felt he owed Stan a confidence in return.

"Sometimes, there's salvage rights on wrecks. It's part of the harbour perks. That's why boatmen can get narky with each other. It's always been that way. You got to keep in with the right people."

"Tell me about it," said Stan. "Same in the Navy. No barrels of rum stashed down there now, I don't suppose?"

Joe smiled. "Not this week. Not as far as I know. Ask me no questions, I won't tell you no lies."

They clambered out into the quiet evening air, and sauntered down the road until they were back in sight of the sea. Halfway down Victoria Road, they were stopped by a man in his early twenties walking the other way. He was dressed in a smart checked jacket. A paisley cravat was tucked into a striped collared shirt at his throat.

"It's young Joe, isn't it?" said the young man as their paths crossed. He sounded as posh as he looked. "My, you've grown a bit since last year…"

"Oh hallo, Mr Le Mesurier," Joe answered shyly. "How are you?"

"Fine, thank you," said the man.

There was a pause.

"Well, I *say* I'm fine," he continued, "But actually I'm only here for a day or so before I report for army duty at Tidworth up on Salisbury Plain. They're going to have me driving tanks. So I suppose I don't know what to make of that. What d'you reckon, Joe? Will I be any good?"

"Well, I've seen you driving a sports car, and you looked all right in that. But wouldn't you rather have joined the Navy like Stan here?"

Mr Le Mesurier laughed. "Oh, I don't think so. Boats are just a bit of fun for me. I was in the army cadets at Sherborne school, so I suppose that's why the army thought I'd fit in. Anyway, thing is, I really ought to see your dad before I go. How's the *Wagtail* coming along? I'd hoped we'd be down for a bit of a romp this summer, but it looks like chance would be a fine thing now."

"We've cleaned her up really nice," said Joe. "She looks great. You can have a look tomorrow morning if you want. "

"That sounds splendid. If I brought June with me, would we find your dad down on the front? About ten?"

"Likely as not," said Joe. "There's not much to do at the moment. We're sitting on our hands."

"I suppose so," said Mr Le Mesurier. "Can't be much fun for Wally. Should think it's driving him bonkers. Perhaps I'll see you tomorrow then…"

And he strolled on, with a wave of his hand.

"Who's he?" asked Stan. "Bit of a toff!"

"That's John Le Mesurier. He says he's an actor, but I've never seen him in any films. Comes down from London at the weekends. Most summers there's a few of his sort around. They like to play at being sailors. Brings us in a bit of cash during the winter, keeping their yachts in trim. Dad says they give him earache, always wanting to yack on about the sea."

That night Joe was woken by the wailing of the air-raid

sirens. There was one high on a pole, nearby on the corner of Albion Place, so in the Camden Square houses the sound was deafening. He checked the time. His watch said one in the morning. Joe found he was trembling as he hurriedly swapped his pyjamas for dayclothes, all fingers and thumbs as he tried to button his trousers. It was the first time the sirens had sounded at night since the false alarms the previous September. Since then, even when they'd gone off during the day it had only been for tests.

When he ran downstairs, the others were already in the kitchen. The kettle was on the gas, and Flo seemed to be making a cup of tea. She was still in her dressing gown and curlers, and was putting on a brave face.

"I'm off up to *Fervent*," declared Stan. "Just in case. But I might be back in half an hour. Who knows? Should you have the gas on, if there really is an air raid, Mrs Read?"

Flo shook her head in annoyance, and fluttered her hands as if she now didn't know what to do. Then she said "Oh, fiddle," and went on making the tea anyway.

"What about us, Dad?" asked Joe, when Stan had left. He knew that although the materials for an Anderson shelter had arrived two months ago, his dad hadn't done anything about building it yet. The corrugated iron and bricks were still stacked against the garden wall. "Are we going to walk over to the Queen Street shelters?"

"Not if I can help it," Wally said gruffly. "Do you want to

spend the night in other people's stink? These public shelters are all very well, but just think about it. A thousand people crowded together with one lav, no privacy and no ventilation. No thank you very much. Let's just sit tight and see what happens, shall we?"

Flo stopped pouring the tea. For the first time she showed some agitation.

"Might be too late by then, Wal," she said, a bit sharply.

Joe's dad tutted, and opening the front door, made a show of listening to whatever might be up there in the night sky. Joe watched from the door as his father climbed the steps into the square and listened again.

"Well, there's planes droning away somewhere," he said, coming back down. "But it don't sound as if they're anywhere close."

"Shut the door then," said Flo. "You're letting all the warmth out."

As she spoke, and before Wally had time to do as she'd asked, there was suddenly a tremendous series of crashing explosions seemingly almost on top of their heads, and the sound of tiles and other debris tumbling and breaking onto the hard surfaces of the pavement and road.

Joe jumped, Flo's hand went to her mouth. Wally swore violently and instinctively banged the door shut behind him.

The three of them spent the rest of a sleepless night taking

turns between the cupboard under the stairs and a makeshift
– but probably completely useless – shelter cobbled together
from the kitchen table and various chairs and cushions. But
thankfully, there was no repeat of the sudden explosion, and
at about four o'clock, the all-clear sounded.

"All right, all right, Flo," said an exasperated Wally at one
point, tired of having his ear bent, "I'll spend tomorrow
making a start on the Anderson. Now put a sock in it, won't
you, and let's try to get some shut-eye."

Thursday 16 May 1940

A caffeine-fuelled, over-excited Stan Wainwright met them over breakfast sometime between seven and eight the next morning.

"False alarm then," he said, far too cheerfully.

"False flippin alarm?" Wally shouted. "Have you seen the roof next door? There's a hole in it the size of the Isle of Wight. You must have walked through a pile of rubbish to get in here. And who d'yer think's going to pay for that? This war's going to be the ruin of this family. Every day seems to bring some new bloody disaster. At this rate we'll all end up sand-scratching for a living."

The Reads owned the next door house, and rented it out.

"Won't the insurance pay?" asked Flo anxiously.

Wally shrugged his shoulders. "Search me!" he said gloomily.

"Sorry, Mr Read," apologised Stan, realizing his lack of tact. "What I meant to say was, good thing it wasn't an air raid."

"So then, clever clogs, what was it then that was so much better than an air raid?" snapped Wally.

"Well, apparently, it were Jerry planes laying mines offshore," said Stan confidentially. "And then what happened was, our destroyers fired off some rounds at the Jerries, and there was like, a bit of collateral damage."

"Collateral damage? Is that what you call it? Putting a hole in our roof. And tell me, young man, did they manage to bring down any of these so-and-so Nazi so-and-so planes?"

"Not so far confirmed, no."

"So they missed, is what you're saying. But somehow managed not to miss Camden Square." Wally paused heavily. "So that's where I'm sending the bill, Flo. Up with young Hornblower here to *H.M.S. Flaming Fervent*."

Stan went rather quiet, as the effects of a night without sleep began to kick in. It was easy to forget, in the office up at *Fervent*, what war meant for ordinary people.

Flo changed the subject. There was a tone of voice she used, slightly higher-pitched than usual, and a bit slower, whenever she was trying out an idea she wasn't sure would fly.

"I was talking to Elsie…" she began. Elsie was Flo's best friend, who lived the other side of Camden Square. "…And Elsie said they're making plans to evacuate all the kids out of harm's way. To Staffordshire they think…"

"Well," grunted Wally, "I should think last night'll help the thought along."

"And I was wondering, Joe…" Flo continued, "If it had

been a year ago, you'd have been going with them, even if it'd only been for a short while … because you'd have still been at school…"

Joe got her drift, and didn't like it. "You're not packing me off somewhere I don't know anybody and no one knows me…" he interrupted, startled and worried at the suggestion. "I won't go."

"No, hear me out, Joe sweetheart," Flo answered. "I was just thinking about your Auntie Rose. You could always go there if you wanted. Jerry surely won't be interested in bombing her."

Joe's Auntie Rose lived in Rye, over the border in Sussex. She and her husband Will had a smallholding and nursery there, on the edge of the pretty little town. Rye was a place with a seafaring history too, though of a different sort to Ramsgate's. If smuggling was an occasional hobby in the Kentish town, at various times long ago it had been Rye's whole life.

Joe's mum Daisy had been ill for a long time before she'd finally died when Joe was just eleven. Joe's brother and sister were much older than he was, and Joe, like Wally, had taken his mum's illness hard. At times back then, especially when Daisy was in hospital, the house in Camden Square had been almost silent. Wally and Joe had retreated into their own shells, using all their energy to survive, emerging only to work and eat the food Joe's sister Nora put in front of them.

During those years, trips to see Auntie Rose, Daisy's sister, had been a lifeline. Joe liked the messiness of life at the smallholding. He could get dirty and no one told him off. He could play and forget that sad things were happening back home. Everyone knew Rose in Rye, and because everyone knew her, everyone knew Joe too, and everyone was kind to him, because they knew why he was there. Joe hadn't been to Rye in a while, and Flo's idea was tempting. Rose always made him feel special.

"Thing is," Flo was saying, "I've had a word with her. All we have to do is walk down the telephone box to say you're coming. Rose'd love to see you. Why not go for a couple of days this weekend, and have a think…"

"Dad?" asked Joe.

"There's nothing to do here, son. I couldn't blame you. There's a lot of folk talking about getting out of Ramsgate, and I don't just mean nippers. Every day you hear about another business shutting down. The place is on its last legs, if you ask me."

"But why, Dad? Why does everyone want to leave?"

"Ramsgate's in the wrong place," said Stan. "There's us Navy types all over the town like a rash, and there's the RAF up at Manston just a couple of miles away. If Jerry ends up in France, and I'm not saying he will, then any planes he sends to attack London'll pass right overhead. This place could become Bomb Alley."

"But everyone says the war'll be over by Christmas."

"I wouldn't count on it…"

"So you reckon I should go too, Stan?"

"Like Flo says, no harm in going to have a look-see…"

Friday 17 May 1940

It took three hours, more or less, to make the journey to Rye. There was a change of trains at Ashford, a wait on Ashford station between the two, and even then the Hastings train didn't exactly hurry its way to Sussex. Joe hadn't been in that direction since war had broken out, and he saw it with different, more adult eyes now. The countryside looked deceptively the same as it had always done – fields of lush green grass dotted with sheep and cows, orchards with blossom-laden trees, white-painted clapboard oast-houses here and there. But having tasted real hard work under his dad's watching, critical eye, he now saw what he'd not seen before – the sheer amount of toil it took to keep the countryside beautiful and well-ordered. He thought about the cold early mornings the farmers must spend milking the cows, the worries there'd be about the size of the next season's crop of apples, the back-breaking labour and skill where there were fields to be ploughed and planted, the incomers from London who'd (perhaps) still be required to pick the hops later in the summer. But then again, maybe this summer, they wouldn't. If his dad and Stan were right.

Ashford station had changed too. It had always been a major railway centre, a fascinating place to be, where worn-out engines and carriages came to be stripped down and made as good as new. Joe had always thought that if he couldn't follow his dad onto the boats, the railway sheds at Ashford would be a good place to work. Now everything looked slightly more shabby than before. On this dull morning there were piles of sandbags on the platform sides, and soldiers milling around the platforms with their tin hats and kitbags. The soldiers seemed at the same time both aimless and as if they owned the place. They jostled the civilians, overpowering them with their mateyness, their chain-smoking and their sheer numbers. It was a relief to Joe when his train finally turned up, twenty minutes late, and he could escape. Even then, the compartment was mostly full of khaki boys puffing away, going on to Hastings, although from their rude, boisterous talk he couldn't make out what they were going to do.

Auntie Rose hadn't changed a bit though. She threw down her gardening gloves to be as welcoming as she'd always been, and Joe found her hugs and kisses just as embarrassing as he remembered.

"I'm earthing up some spuds," she said. "Want to come and help?" So within five minutes of arriving, Joe found himself with filthy hands, ankle deep in rich Sussex soil, heaping up the mounds of loam that in a couple of months' time would produce treasure chests of potatoes. As they worked, they talked about family things, about what life was like in Ramsgate, about his dad's worries. They laughed too, as they remembered the times Joe had enjoyed among the pigs and chickens when he was a little boy.

Before she'd met Wally and fallen in love with the widowed seaman who'd so amused her with his sailor's tales, Flo's home had been in London. Her cooking was basic, and apart from the constant supply of fresh fish, she tended to fall back on tins as an easy way out. Food rationing was getting to be a problem for Flo. On the other hand Rose was a real countrywoman – she even had a Sussex accent now – and the food she served mostly came from what she and Will grew or kept. Tonight it was roast chicken with three kinds of fresh vegetables, and apple pie with home-made custard to follow. Compared with the usual Camden Square menu, it was a feast.

"What do you think?" Rose said gently to Joe over a mug of cocoa when they'd finished eating. "Would you like to come and live here for a while? You'd be a great help, you know. It wouldn't be charity."

Joe stirred the cocoa, and studied the milky circles in the foam on its top, as if he was going to find an answer there. "I dunno," he anwered. "Maybe…"

Saturday 18 May 1940

The next morning Rose asked Joe if he'd walk into Rye and collect some things from the grocery store and the chemist's shop. Joe wandered around the lanes, through Church Square and up Mermaid Street. Everything was all so perfectly pretty, with the black and white half-timbering and cobbles. And quiet too! There was nothing like the bustle and energy of Ramsgate. Just a few people were up and about, raising their hats to each other, stopping to exchange a few polite words. One or two cars pootled sedately along the roads, tyres rumbling. But then, that wasn't at all surprising. Rye was off the beaten track, which was exactly what would make it so safe for however long the war continued. The quays and the rivers which flowed into one another around the town were equally tranquil. Compared with the tangle of traffic in the broad expanse of Ramsgate's harbour, here there were a few nice little boats, carefully arranged at their moorings, and not a naval uniform in sight.

They whiled away Saturday, weeding the vegetable patches carefully so as not to pull up the vegetables with the weeds, feeding the animals, and petting the two bedraggled donkeys kind-hearted Rose had taken in because there was no work for them on the beaches at Camber Sands this year. Rose said nothing more to Joe about coming to live in Rye, even though Joe was due to catch the nine o'clock Sunday train back to Ashford.

"Everything all right then?" Rose asked as they walked together silently down to the station. Joe had said almost nothing all morning, bar a few grunts. But then, he was fifteen. What else could you expect?

"I do miss your mum," she said suddenly. "She'd have known what you should do. And she'd have told you too, straight out."

Joe offered no comment.

"I'd love to come and stay with you and Uncle Will," he said eventually, when they were almost at the station yard. He stopped and looked at her. "But I don't think it'd be right. I should be with my dad. What if something bad happened? If I was here, I'd be worrying all the time. I belong with him, however tough it gets. Otherwise, later, I'd know I'd chickened out. Wouldn't I?"

"I think that's lovely. And brave," said Rose. "Your mum'd have been proud of you. You've got to do what you think's best, Joe. Just take care, that's all, and don't take too much on yourself. You're young and you've only got one life, remember."

41

Sunday 19 May 1940

Because it was Sunday, the journey back to Ramsgate took even longer. It was nearly two o' clock before Joe walked into Camden Square.

"Only me at home," said Flo. "No idea where Stan is, and your dad's out on a shout with the *Prudential*. Tom came for him 'bout midday, and said they was short-handed. No peace for the wicked. Actually, I'm glad to get him out from under my feet. He's that fed up with having nothing to do. Between you and me, I think he's letting it all get to 'im. When you think about it, we're in clover compared to most. Ignore that stuff about sand-scratching ... you'll never catch *your* dad scrabbling along the beach, looking for bric-a-brac to flog off. We could scrape by on the rent from the houses, if we had to. So whatever else, Joe sweetheart, don't go worrying your head about that!"

Joe wandered down to the lifeboat station. He found Fred Liddle sitting outside sprawled in a canvas chair, dragging on a cigarette, looking fidgety and ill at ease. Fred was usually a regular on the *Prudential*, but maybe he'd been too slow reacting that morning, and hadn't made it there in time for the shout. Probably on the beer the previous night.

"What's up, Fred?" Joe called.

"Some Navy drifter's only gorn and flippin' hit a sandbank. I mean, young Joe, not jest grounded herself, but flippin' *rammed* it by all accounts. They don't understand, these Navy fellers. Jest because it says on their charts there's clear water one day, don't mean to say it's gonna be the same the next. It's book-learning that's the trouble, if y'ask me. They never stop to ask. Not once have I 'ad a conversation with one of their blokes 'bout sand or tides or nothin'. Thinks they knows it all."

Joe had been brought up with the lore of the Goodwin Sands. It was quite true. The sands shifted day to day. Sometimes you could go out, gently beach a boat, clamber out, and play a game of cricket. Go back to the very same place a day later, and you might be staring at a fifteen-foot cliff of sand, so if there was fog around, the unwary could easily be in trouble. Countless ships had foundered in the area: two *thousand*, some said.

"Where is she?" asked Joe.

"Down near the *Stirling Castle*, according to the Navy lads. Should have left 'em to sort out their own mess, if you ask me, but they said they were shorthanded, so could we deal with it. Flippin' cheek. No doubt when we fetch 'em off they'll say they saw the *Lovibond* an' all."

The *Stirling Castle* was a famous naval ship of the

seventeenth century, sunk in the Great Storm of 1703. And the *Lovibond* was a schooner wrecked deliberately by its first mate because of his jealousy for the captain's wife. Locals said the ghost of the ship returned every fifty years to the place of its downfall. Both ships made regular appearances in the tales Wally Read told to those who sailed with them on the *New Britannic*.

Back in the old days of his great-uncle Tom, Joe would have probably already been out with the lifeboat by now, in view of his size and strength. But these days, there were more rules, and he'd have to be seventeen before they even considered him, or so the new coxswain said. If Old Tom had still been in charge, he'd have turned a blind eye but Howard Primrose Knight, besides being a very good seaman, was a stickler for doing things right. If they thought Howard was going too far, the other boatmen called him '*Primrose*' behind his back, but they couldn't really even tease him for that. He'd been given the name in memory of a sailor famously rescued by the Ramsgate boat long ago. In Ramsgate's harbour traditions, the Knights went back at least as far as the Reads.

It was late afternoon before the *Prudential* returned, with the drifter and its rather shame-faced crew in tow.

"Well, was that a so-and-so to free off!" Wally exclaimed, as he bullocked through the door of number 38. "Little boat, big trouble!"

"Everyone OK, Wal?" asked Flo.

"Yeah, of course," he replied. "I mean, we shouldn't be doin' stuff like that! S'pose it's better than sitting on our arses, though."

"Not another *Dunbar Castle* then, Dad?" Joe laughed.

"Not exactly, no, son! And we don't want many more of those, neither. That was a day and a half, I can tell yer!"

In January that year the ten-thousand ton *Dunbar Castle* had hit a mine off the East Cliff when she was carrying all sorts of cargo and people to Cape Town in South Africa. A hundred and forty-odd people were pulled off, including a party of nuns, but ten of the crew hadn't made it, some of them killed in the explosion which sent her down. A valuable race-horse which was on board wasn't so lucky either: it was never going to survive the chaos. The sand-scratchers had a real field-day after that one. All kinds of things were washed up: leather cushions, carpets, chairs, and even a grand piano, though it wasn't in a fit state to be played. The wreck was still out there, while they decided what to do with her.

"Weren't they going to blow the *Dunbar* up, Dad?" Joe asked.

"Still thinking about it, son. They're worried they'll take out half of the windows in Ramsgate if they do."

You didn't get any of this kind of stuff in Rye.

A while later, Stan came in and together they settled down with a cup of tea to listen to the news.

"I don't know that I wants to, Flo," said Wally. "Whatever

45

it is it won't be good."

But they turned the wireless on anyway. Wally was right. There wasn't much to cheer you up, and what followed was even worse. That week, Britain had found itself a new Prime Minister. His name was Winston Churchill, and the way you heard people talk about him he was the best of a bad bunch. They thought he was unreliable and hot-headed. They didn't think for a moment that he'd be able to hold the Parliament and the country together. They thought he'd be blown away by the next really bad bit of news. Now at last, thanks to the miracle of the wireless, everyone could hear his voice.

"I speak to you for the first time as Prime Minister in a solemn hour for the life of our country, of our empire, of our allies, and above all, of the cause of Freedom," he said. "A tremendous battle is raging in France and Flanders. The Germans, by a remarkable combination of air-bombing and heavily-armed tanks, have broken through the French defences, and strong columns of their armoured vehicles are ravaging the open country. They have penetrated deeply, and spread alarm and confusion in their track…"

And then towards the end of his ten-minute speech he went on:

"After this battle in France, there will come the battle for our island – for all that Britain is, and all that Britain means. That will be the struggle… Today is Trinity Sunday. Centuries ago words were written to be a call and a spur to the faithful servants of Truth and Justice: 'Arm yourselves and be ye men of valour; for it is better for us to perish in battle than to look upon the outrage of our nation and our altar. As the Will of God is in Heaven, even so let it be.'"

When the speech was ended, there was silence on the radio for a moment, and in the silence, with a nod from Wally, Joe switched the wireless off. No one spoke for a few moments. Then Wally said, "Well, that explains a couple of things then."

"What's that?"

"Firstly, why the King's said there's to be a National Day of Prayer next Sunday, 'cos I reckon that's about all we've got left. And secondly why, when we were out on the Goodwins this afternoon we could hear the bloomin' guns. They never let up all afternoon. And there were planes over the Channel like a swarm of gnats."

"Do you reckon it's that bad?" asked Flo. Joe could see the pale, delicate skin on her face even whiter than usual in the late afternoon light filtering through the window.

"I was going to say something anyway," said Stan. "I can't tell you much, like, but there's a complete flap on up at *Fervent*. Basically the word is the French are a basket case. Worse than I let on the other day. No-one's coming right out with it, but I reckon Jerry'll be at the Channel ports in no time. Days rather than weeks. After that, well, work it out for yourself. It'll be us next. And once they're on the Frenchies'

47

airfields those Nazi bombers are ten minutes away."

Joe had never seen Flo cry before. She wasn't generally the crying sort. But she was off on one now, her shoulders heaving, her hanky soaked. She blew her nose loudly, and looked pathetically up at Wally from where she was sitting.

"I don't think I can take no more, Wal," she sobbed. "What with the bloomin'war, then Ivy, and no money coming in. And now, according to Stan, we're all going to be blown to bits by the Jerries, and if we get through that, murdered in our beds. There's no food to be had, and what are they going to ration next, I ask you? 1/10d for a ration of meat don't buy more than a chicken leg each."

Wally shifted uneasily from foot to foot. He was good at doing things, he'd help you out in times of trouble, but you wouldn't go to Walter Read if you wanted advice or comfort. He didn't know how to act with a woman when she did this. He never had, not with Daisy, not even in her worst moments, and not now.

"And sugar," Flo wailed on. "You like your tea, but you can't abide it without a mountain of sugar, so where's twelve ounces going to go in a week?"

"You'll manage, love," was the best Wally could offer, in a mumbling kind of way.

"I couldn't manage, Wal. Not if anything were to happen to you. Suppose the Huns took you away. Or suppose you did what you said, and tried to fight them coming up the beach, and then they shot you?"

Wally shrugged his shoulders.

"Ifs and maybes," he said. "Let's just worry about today, shall we?"

But Flo couldn't do that.

Monday 20 May 1940

Joe could see Flo still hadn't fully recovered when they all went down to *The Queen's Head* early the next evening for a pint or two and a lemonade, the three of them along with Bill Matthews and his wife Gertrude. They sat outside. Today, everyone could hear the guns – dull explosions and rumbles that on another day they might have written off as distant thunder. Some of the people looking out over the harbour had binoculars or telescopes, but visibility wasn't good, and they couldn't see anything for certain on the water's far side. Occasional aircraft flying into or out of RAF Manston passed overhead singly or in flights of four or five – Blenheims, Spitfires and Hurricanes. As the planes soared past and out over the Channel, the occupants of the pub stood up, waved and cheered, yelling at them to 'Give Jerry hell'. Joe felt better, being in a crowd. It gave him courage. That afternoon he and Wally had been out cautiously fishing off the Sands in *Bulldog*, their little smack. They hadn't caught much, a few flat fish, a few bass, some herrings, not enough of anything to make a worthwhile sale, and all the while he and Wally had been almost wordless. It made no difference. The fish still stayed away, despite the silence.

A man in a suit rounded the corner and came up to them.

"Ah, Read," he said to Wally in a self-important kind of way. "I was hoping I'd find you about. How are you keeping?"

Wally looked up lazily, his hand still on his pint. He pushed back his cap, but didn't stand up, as the stranger might have been expecting or hoping, given the number of people there were around.

"*Alderman* Kempe," he said, with heavy emphasis on the title, "I'm well enough, considering. How's life up in the council offices? They keeping you busy up there?"

"I should say," said the Mayor of Ramsgate, wondering if etiquette demanded that he bought Wally a drink. "What with the usual civic business, and liaising with the Navy, it's all quite a challenge, I can tell you! This can't be your boy, Walter? Didn't recognize him, he's grown so much."

Joe scowled. He didn't think too much of Mr Kempe.

"So what can I do for you then?" said Wally, cutting to the chase. He didn't want to waste valuable drinking time yakking to the high and mighty Alderman.

"Thing is ... it's *that* time of the year again..."

"Oh yes...?"

"And I know circumstances are a trifle ... *difficult* ... but there are a few people I'd like to take out on the *Britannic* for

51

an hour or so. If that was all right with you…"

Wally said nothing, to encourage what might come next.

"Of course, I'd be happy to make a contribution to expenses. I know times are hard…"

"Well, so they are, Mr Kempe, and that's very handsome of you, I'm sure. And I suppose you'll want to do a spot of fishing?"

The only time the *New Britannic* was ever set to a fishing expedition was this one occasion a year for the Mayor and his cronies. Wally and Bill would sling a trawl net over the side, to see what they could come up with, and the Mayor raffled off the results to his guests. Wally was coming to think of the annual outing as a sort of unofficial tax. It was a flippin' nuisance, because every inch of the boat had to be scrubbed and disinfected each time afterwards, and even then the smell hung around. Mind you, the regular punters never knew, did they? Thought it was just a real healthy whiff of the sea or 'ozone' or something equally daft.

"Not this year. Just a ride. Would Friday afternoon be convenient? Say four p.m.? I'll have a caterer send down some food, if you can arrange for some beer in the usual way."

It was short notice, but the deal was done.

"You OK with that then, Bill?" Wally asked.

"It's a living, ain't it, Wal? Silly beggars can't be choosers, these days!"

Bill was a taller man than Wally though about the same

age, in his mid-forties, with rather less hair, well muscled and strong. When Wally was off doing other things, which was quite often in a normal year, Bill was left in charge of the *New Britannic*. In high season they needed at least two and sometimes three crew on board to look after the passengers and the bar. There was never any shortage of volunteers to help out.

They settled back in their chairs after the Mayor's departure, and Bill gazed out to sea.

"I often wonder what Arthur's getting up to over there," he murmured wistfully. "I hope the boy's all right." Arthur was Bill's younger brother. Joe had heard many times how he was in France with the British Expeditionary Force.

"I was that proud when he joined the Buffs," Bill went on. The Buffs were the Royal East Kent Regiment. "But now how I wish to God he hadn't, and I sometimes think, will we ever see him again?"

Flo was reminding herself to be grateful for small mercies. At least she didn't have family serving in France. She put a hand on Gertrude's arm.

"Artie's a fine young man," she said. "He'll be back, mark my words. Don't you worry, Gert."

Good thing Gert hadn't seen Flo yesterday evening, Joe thought. But that was the way it was. You were up one minute, and then down the next. You looked after each other.

Flo changed the subject. "Any business at the B & B this

year, Gert?" she asked.

"Bits and bobs," Gert answered. "There's a woman staying this week till Saturday morning. Down from London and *says* she's havin' a holiday, but don't look much like it to me. Apart from that, no one's exactly beating a path to our door."

"Gert should talk to Stan, shouldn't she, Wal? He might get her some business. We done all right from our Navy boys. Lovely lads!"

But Gert wasn't listening. She was still going on about her current house guest.

"I mean, she's dressed up like she's going to an office. Hair done up, smart skirt, heels. Asking questions like there's no tomorrow." She dropped her voice to a stage whisper. "And bless my soul, if that isn't her now. Would you just look at that!"

A small, neat, youngish woman, dressed as Gert had described, walked past, head held high, straight into the lounge bar of *The Queen's Head*. Either she'd ignored them or just hadn't seen them. Either way, it was a bit odd. You didn't get women on their own in Ramsgate pubs.

"No better than she should be!" Gert exclaimed, and then continued, "I'll tell you something else for free. She signs herself '*Hilde*' with an 'e' at the end. Speaks with a cut glass accent all right, but you could make that up, couldn't you? I reckon she's foreign. Might even be a Jerry."

"What you saying, Gert?" said Bill sharply. "Steady on there, girl. You're not suggesting she's a spy?"

"How would we know? I'm just saying it all seems odd to me."

Wednesday 22 May 1940

"Anyone been to see your dad about the *New Britannic* yet?" Stan asked.

He and Joe were down by the Pavilion sharing the lunchtime jam sandwiches Flo had made. There was a fretful, squally wind, and dampness in the air. Stan was glad to be out in the open, away from his stuffy office. Joe had been up since seven scraping muck off the bottom of a dirty old smack with his dad and Bill, and needed a breather.

"Yeah, one of your lot was poking around yesterday. Tall bloke, dark hair, with a briefcase and funny ears. Wanted to see her. Wrote some things down."

"Sounds like my boss. Chief Petty Officer Cawdron. His ears got that way playing rugby. They make me feel funny looking at them. He's all right though. Did he say anything interesting?"

"'*Nice little boat,*' and that was about it. Said he'd be in touch. Was sure we '*would be of great assistance at some point*'."

"Like I said, something's going off, and it's something big," said Stan. "As far as the likes of the *New Britannic's*

56

concerned, first they were just thinking about clearing mines, but now it's bigger than that. You've got to ask yourself, if there are all those soldiers stuck in France – hundreds of thousands old Cawdron reckons – and Jerry's closing in, how the heck are they going to get 'em home? Might be all hands on deck..."

Joe was suddenly distracted. "There's that woman again," he said, pointing across the quay. She was wearing a headscarf and dark glasses, but even so, he was sure it was the same person.

"What woman?"

"The one I told you about. The one who was in *The Queen's Head* two nights ago. The one Gert says is called Hilde."

"Oh, her. She's being a bit nosey, in't she?"

The woman had field glasses and a canvas bag slung round her neck. Every now and then she took a notebook and pencil from the bag, and jotted something down. Then the notebook went back in the bag, and she raised the binoculars to look at something else.

"Well, if she's not a spy, like Gert thinks, she's certainly acting like one. What should we do?" Joe was quite excited.

"She's not going to run very far or fast in them heels," said Stan. "Let's just keep an eye on her for a bit."

As the woman moved around the harbour, they moved with her, keeping their distance. She went along the front to the west side, heading in the direction of the lifeboat station. Every now and then, she seemed to make an excuse to stop a passer-by. Twice it happened, and both times there was a conversation which continued for a few minutes before she moved on. After the second conversation, the notebook came out again, and she wrote down more details, balancing the book on her knee.

"There's my Uncle Tom," said Joe. Tom was trudging his way over to the lifeboat station, hands in pockets. He was probably off to do some maintenance on the *Prudential*. "I wonder if she'll stop to talk to him?" And sure enough she did. They swapped words for a few moments, though it was obvious from Tom's manner that he hadn't got time for idle chat.

"Let's go and ask him what she wanted to know," said Stan, when Hilde set off again. Tom had turned. He watched Hilde's back as she walked away. Then he resumed his trudge, pulling off his cap and scratching his head.

"Tell the truth, young Joe, I don't know what she wanted," he muttered when they caught up with him. "Asked did I work on the lifeboat, and had we been on many shouts recently, and what for, and were the mines a problem. I didn't let on much, but she still asked if she could come back and talk to me again."

"You might not want to do that, Mr Read," said Stan, "She's acting a bit suspicious, like. We're wondering if she's up to no good. Perhaps you should tell the police. Or I should pass it on to our lot."

"Well she don't look like no Mata Hari," Tom answered. "And I don't reckon it'd help Jerry to know what the *Prudential* gets up to. But maybe you're right … it's Stan isn't it? I've heard about you from Wally."

Stan wondered what exactly he'd heard. Walter Read still seemed as suspicious of him as Joe was of Hilde. Any road, the lady had moved on to do her espionage somewhere else now. Or perhaps just gone to eat a late lunch. Should he do anything? Best tell C.P.O. Cawdron, he thought. Just in case.

Friday 24 May 1940

Alderman Kempe was feeling pleased with life today. On the one hand who knew what the future might hold, and on the other, the past few weeks had been a blur of confused activity with not much sleep and meals snatched here and there, but today ... today was going to be good. Even the weather was doing its bit. The rain had scurried away, the sky over the English Channel was a deep blue, the wind was blowing gently from the south west, and the temperature was climbing quickly. Today might be the one real day of summer this year, and he was going to make the best of it.

He liked entertaining: it was one of the best parts of his job, and he was good at it too. 'Working the room', an American acquaintance had once called it, by which his Yankee friend had meant making sure that you talked to everyone at a function, that you made sure they were all enjoying themselves, and most importantly, they all knew who *you* were, and what you wanted of them.

And today what he had in mind was an act of defiance. It was, after all, for the time being as it always had been, the *English* Channel. He and his friends were going to celebrate that while they could. He liked the song that had been so popular from the end of last year, particularly the version sung by that pretty young girl, Vera Lynn. Pity he couldn't have got *her* to come down and join them. His wife had bought the sheet music, and she played it on the piano for him at home from time to time while they sang together: *'There'll always be an England, and England shall be free...'* He'd intended to hold today's reception in the Mayor's Parlour at the council offices, but then at the last minute it had suddenly come to him that he was blowed if he was going to give in to the Germans and if they could, they should spend an hour or so on Walter's Read's boat.

He loved Ramsgate, and everything it stood for, even though he'd only lived there for eight years. One of the things that kept him awake at nights was the thought that the place might finally go down the pan while he was still Mayor. It wasn't his fault, of course it wasn't – he couldn't prevent a war that was being driven by a despotic madman – but he didn't want the history books to show that Ramsgate had gone to the dogs on his watch. Take chaps like poor Walter Read, for instance. Good man, even if he ducked and dived a bit, and kept his cash under the floorboards, away from the taxman. But this year suddenly there was probably little to put in Walter's cashbox, and no immediate possibility of that situation improving. So the Mayor's message for today was that Ramsgate was open for business. He'd invited the town's great and good, like Admiral Evans and Lady Richborough. With them would be those who'd stood shoulder to shoulder with him during the last couple of years, like Mr Brimmell his borough engineer, who'd supported him so valiantly while together they'd pestered the government for the money to have air-raid shelters dug in the chalk. Harold Balfour, the local M.P., had promised to try to be there – and wasn't he an inspiration! The chap knew all about war – he'd been a fighter ace in the Great War, when just going up in an aeroplane was to take your life into your hands. Now he had an important job in the Air Ministry, yet still he took the time to be a proper Member of Parliament. Balfour knew the area and its people all right, and seemed to care about them.

Some of the Alderman's invitations had been regretfully declined of course. He'd tried to get the Duke of Kent to come down, but the Duke had written to say he was sorry – he had a previous engagement. The Alderman had chortled to find he'd had better luck with Cosmo Lang, the Archbishop of Canterbury, who'd telephoned to say he'd be delighted. He was in Canterbury that day and there was a gap in his diary, but if it was all right with Alderman Kempe, could he come in mufti and leave his bishop's garb at home – apart from a simple dog-collar, of course? Then there were a few journalists, including some from national newspapers like the *Daily Express*. Very important that, if you wanted to get your message across. One of them had been here for a week, talking to people, and finding out what it was like *on Britain's new front-line*.

Alderman Kempe put on his best clothes, including his trademark frock coat and top hat, adjusted the chain around his neck, and went out into the sunshine to check that everything was in order for the day.

"Funny thing," said Bill Matthews to Wally and Joe, as they were tidying up the *New Britannic*, and helping Alderman Kempe's caterers carry crates of food aboard, "A knock comes on the door when I'm just finishing my breakfast this morning, and blow me, there's only a copper standing on the doorstep. Says to Gert is it right we've got a lodger this week, and if so can he have a word with her. Gert answers yes but she's gone off to have her hair done in town, so the copper says, when will she back then and Gert says she really doesn't know, and then the copper says would that be at Harvey's then, and Gert says well she supposes so, she looks as if she can afford it. And then the copper goes off towards town. So what do you make of that?"

"Sounds like someone other than Gert thinks your lady lodger might be a spy, that's what," chuckled Wally. "Hope Gert let on she had her suspicions. Otherwise they'll 'ave you for aiding and abetting, or givin' comfort to the enemy or some such!"

"Get away! Mind you, I don't think Gert said nothing, 'part from showing him the woman's name in the register.

If the police are on to this Hilde woman, best let them sort it out."

Joe listened, and said nothing, but felt rather proud. He'd told Stan where the Matthews family lived up in Bloomsbury Road. Sounded like their information about Hilde had been passed on. He wondered vaguely to himself whether they'd all get medals if she really did turn out to be a Jerry spy.

The guests sauntered down to the harbour with Alderman Kempe at the front of the little crocodile, accompanied by a grey-haired man in a clerical collar and a deep purple shirt.

"The Archbishop of flippin' Canterbury!" Walter muttered to Joe as they waited to embark the little queue at the quayside. "Whatever will old man Kempe think of next? Does he think we need good luck for the voyage? Let's hope the Archbishop don't decide to try walking on water! If he does, perhaps he'd like to take Mr Kempe with 'im!"

There were about fifty in the party. Even with all the food and drink and the waitresses, who at the moment were fussing they'd lose their caps in the breeze, there'd be plenty of room on board the *Britannic* today.

When the last person had received a helping hand up the little gangplank and over the side into the boat, Alderman Kempe checked his watch anxiously.

"A couple more still to arrive, I think, Walter. Ah, here they are…"

Half running up the quayside came a young sandy-haired

man wearing a sports jacket. Slightly behind him, clutching a sun hat to her head, was a smartly dressed woman in sunglasses and heels, with a nice new hairdo. Hilde!

Joe looked, didn't believe what he saw at first, and then looked again. First of all he was indignant that a Jerry spy should have the nerve to gatecrash the Mayor's party. And then it began to dawn that something was wrong here...

"Hello, Ken," welcomed the Mayor. "Better late than never..."

"Sorry Mr Kempe," said the lad. "May I introduce you to Hilde Marchant. I'm afraid Miss Marchant has had a spot of bother today. Some misunderstanding at the police station, apparently. A case of mistaken identity..."

"Lovely to meet you, Miss Marchant," the Mayor said smoothly. "Of course I'm familiar with your work in the *Daily Express*. And the *Picture Post*. Your articles always make such splendid reading. It's a privilege to have you in Ramsgate. I hope you'll be able to carry back some good tales about us to London."

It was hard to tell Hilde Marchant's mood as she said tartly, "Well I'll certainly have *some* tales to tell, Mr Kempe. For some reason, the local police seemed to think I might be a German spy. It's certainly the first time *that*'s ever happened to me. But I suppose we journalists may have to get used to it in the next few months, if we're to do our job properly."

The Mayor clucked and cooed, smoothing any possible

ruffled feathers while Hilde took Joe's hand and stepped into the *Britannic*.

"I've seen you before, haven't I, young man?" she said to him.

"Er ... have you, ma'am?" Joe replied politely, his face reddening, and his eyes shyly downcast. "I don't think so…"

"This is Joe Read, Miss Marchant. His father Walter, owns the *New Britannic*. Anything you want to know about the harbour and the Goodwins, just ask the Read family."

"Yes, I think it was at the harbour that I saw you, wasn't it Joe? Near the lifeboat station? You were with another young man – a naval rating. You seemed to be walking in the same direction as me. *Behind* me, as I recall…"

Joe felt her eyes drilling into him. Did she suspect it was them that had shopped her? At the time she hadn't given the slightest indication that she knew she was being followed.

"Anyway," she said, "Perhaps we can have a chat later, if you're not too busy, and you can tell me what it's like for the younger generation living in Ramsgate in the middle of a war."

Joe muttered something vague, and busied himself with making ready to cast off.

The sea was like a millpond, which from the waitresses' point of view was probably a good thing as they wobbled about the *New Britannic* dispensing cucumber sandwiches and slices of Victoria Sponge to the passengers. There was a buzz of conversation, and Joe's dad, as he'd been asked to, described what there was to be seen, and what had happened through hundreds of years of seafaring. He told the story about the *Lovibond*, though anyone local had heard it a hundred times before. Hilde Marchant had her notebook out and was scribbling away.

They'd been out about three quarters of an hour, when they first heard the sound of a single aircraft, travelling in their direction from the French coast. But it was immediately clear something was wrong. The note of the engine was low, staccato, guttural. Then they could see the plane, low in the sky and still losing height. It was a Hurricane – Joe knew that from the shape – and its engine was faltering, on the verge of cutting out for good, and as it came nearer they could see a burst of angry flame reach out and engulf the cockpit and starboard wing.

The passengers shielded their eyes, and gasped in anxiety and horror.

"Why doesn't the fellow bail out?" someone shouted.

"Too low," muttered Harold Balfour, and even as he said it the pilot lost control of the plane completely. It jagged from side to side before lurching one final time violently to port and nose-diving towards the sea, maybe a mile from where they were. They watched it fall five hundred feet or so and hit the water with a tremendous explosion of water and steam. Hands went to mouths. All conversation stopped.

The sound of the *Britannic's* engine suddenly seemed very loud. The water lapped against its side. Cosmo Lang, the Archbishop, seized the cross on his chest and in the silence asked them if they'd join with him in praying for the safety of the young man inside the plane. But although they did so, in their heart of hearts they knew he hadn't a chance because of the fire and the violence of the plane's impact on the sea. For Joe, who'd seen so many aircraft cavorting around the skies recently and who'd so often wondered what it would be like to have the freedom and fun of all that speed, the horror was like a punch in the stomach. He could only too easily put himself in the place of the young pilot struggling and failing to avoid an early death.

Bill yanked the tiller, and opening up the engines, swung the *New Britannic* round, making as much speed as he could towards the site of the crash. But there was nothing to be done. They could see wreckage spread over an area of a few hundred yards, bits of fuselage and wings blackened and still steaming, but of the plane's pilot not the slightest sign.

"Poor devil," said Alderman Kempe, "God rest his soul."

"He died in a noble cause," said someone else pompously, "In the service of King and Country."

"But just think of his poor family," said someone else quietly.

Hilde Marchant, unobserved by anyone other than Joe, discreetly took her notebook from her bag.

Within ten minutes a fast naval motor boat was on the scene. Wally and its skipper briefly swapped a few words by loud hailer.

"*Hello, New Britannic. Can you confirm you're all OK? Any casualties on board?*"

It might have seemed to the naval boat that there'd been a collision.

"We're fine. No casualties," Wally shouted back.

"*Any survivors from the aircraft?*"

"No survivors that we can see."

It all put rather a dampener on Alderman Kempe's afternoon. Suddenly the war seemed a little closer to everyone on board.

Saturday 25 and Sunday 26 May 1940

An air of gloom hung around Camden Square all weekend, and nothing could shift it. It got to Wally too, although he'd been close to death and the dying countless times. But even he had only rarely seen the moment of someone's passing – usually he got there afterwards – and mostly he'd helped rescue folk caught up in accidents, even if some of them had been caused by sheer stupidity. What they'd witnessed on Friday was sad and horrifying because the victim was so young – most of the pilots were in their early twenties – and was probably the result of enemy action. There wouldn't even be a body for the grieving parents to bury. What if it had been Ernie or Joe?

None of what was said about the tragedy helped Joe much.

"When your number comes up, that's it, isn't it?" Stan had said. Which was OK as far as it went but not exactly comforting. Was that what life was all about then – a lottery?

"He probably didn't know nothin' about it," was all Wally could say in trying to make Joe feel better. And not true, Joe

70

thought, because it was obvious there'd been plenty of time for the young pilot to understand all too clearly what was happening to him.

"Perhaps he bailed out long before we saw him, and got picked up in mid-Channel?" Joe said hopefully. No one answered, and Joe knew pigs might fly before anyone thought *that* had really happened.

Wally didn't find *The Queen's Head* much of a place to be on Saturday evening either. There was always a bit of bad feeling among the boatmen about the Mayor's trips out on the *New Britannic*, a jealous hint here and there that maybe the Reads were too pally with posh folk, even sometimes from those who should have known better, like Coxswain Knight. They didn't mean anything by it – it was just part of the banter of harbour life, but on this occasion Wally didn't want to stay down there to listen to it.

"Are you coming to the service at the Seaman's Chapel tomorrow then, Wal?" Howard Knight asked. "6.30?"

"And why should I want to do that?" Wally asked. He hadn't been inside any kind of church for years apart from family funerals.

"National Day of Prayer," said the Coxswain, who was a regular chapel person, "We think the *Prudential* should put up a show."

"I'll have to see," grumbled Wally. "But I ain't making promises."

"What do you reckon, Flo?" he asked at breakfast on Sunday.

"I think it would be nice," Flo said. "Anyway, far as I can make out, nearly everyone's going to a service somewhere. It'll look a bit funny if we don't put in an appearance. And after all, Wal, you was pilot of the harbour, till you gave it up. Seems only right you should be there."

The little Seaman's Chapel was packed to the rafters with everyone who was anyone in the port of Ramsgate. Even an off-duty Stan had come along, although he'd already been on parade for another service in the morning.

A middle-aged man called Winterburn who was the honorary harbour and lifeboat chaplain led the service. They sang 'O God our help in ages past,' and the seaman's hymn, 'Eternal Father strong to save', and then after a lot of boring prayers the Reverend Winterburn began to speak.

He talked about how God sometimes called people to make sacrifices, and sometimes even to lay down their lives in a great cause. And he said that they were all in that situation now, when everything that was precious about the British way of life was under threat. He spoke of a great disaster about to happen in France. As Joe sat there he felt a hot, burning fear rising up inside him that if there was a God maybe he was going to ask Joe to lay down *his* life. There was nowhere for Joe to escape to: he just had to sit there feeling more and more certain with every second that this really was going to happen. At the end of the service, they all sang the national anthem, and the singing was so loud it seemed that the roof was going to lift off, but Joe was in a terrified daze as they walked out into the sunlight.

"That was really nice," Flo said.

'*Nice?*' thought Joe. It had been anything but nice. Frightening, yes, rousing too in a strange kind of way and definitely patriotic, but in no way *nice*.

"Stupid old bugger of a sky-pilot. What does he know about sacrifice?" said Wally.

"Reminds me of Sundays in Manchester," said Stan, feeling really homesick for the first time in a while.

Apparently unable to stay away from everything to do with Ramsgate, Hilde Marchant had been there at the back of the chapel again, but this time there'd been no notebook on show. Joe had stolen a look at her from time to time, and once spotted her secretly wiping away a tear from the corner of her eye with her hanky. They passed her as they walked out into the street.

"Thank you for showing us the sights on Friday, Mr Read," she said. "I'm so sorry it ended in such an appalling way. I hope we meet again in happier circumstances." She smiled at Joe. "Your son's a fine lad. He's a credit to you. I'm sure we'll hear much more of him."

Joe couldn't imagine why she said that. She was just being polite, he thought, the way posh people did.

Monday 27 May 1940

After the service at the Seaman's Chapel, Stan disappeared. He wasn't at Camden Square for breakfast, and only made a red-eyed, bleary appearance just before tea-time. "Only got ten minutes," he yawned. "Sorry," he added quickly, realizing he was sounding rude. "That came out wrong. It's just that I'm absolutely bushed. But I wanted to grab you while there was the chance, Mr Read. A strong cup of tea would be nice, Flo. Or maybe coffee. I need something to keep me awake. It's going to be another long night."

"What's up, Stan?" asked Joe, yesterday's fears mostly forgotten now. Over the last fortnight, Stan had become a bit of a hero to the younger boy. Stan didn't exactly discourage the idea. As far as Joe was concerned Stan knew everything there was to know about the way the war was going – far better even than Alvar Liddell reading the news on the BBC's Home Service.

"Like we thought, everything's gone completely pear-shaped," said Stan grimly, talking to Wally rather than Joe. "Jerry's steam-rollering the French. Everyone thought they'd put up more of a fight, but it didn't turn out that way at all.

The Frogs pretty much just ran away. Typical! So now they're withdrawing the British Expeditionary Force from France."

"You mean we're retreating, Stan?" Wally grunted. "Running away. Same as the Frogs."

"It's not what they're calling it, but it's the same difference. Anyway, more's the point, our boys are cut off. The way I'm hearing it, three hundred thousand men plus half the Frenchie army are sitting ducks on a narrow strip of land around Dunkirk, with nothing more than a canal or two to prevent the Nazis moving in to finish them off. If they do, then that's our army gone for a burton, and there'll be nothing to stop Hitler invading Britain."

Wally shook his head. He wasn't a military man, but he couldn't see how things could ever have come to this.

"So now we're flat out to get the men off the beaches and back home. We're sending as many warships as we dare, but there are two problems with that. The first is that while they're waiting off the French coast or in Dunkirk they're open to attack by the Luftwaffe. Jerry outnumbers us in the air ten to one – it won't be a contest. And anyway the Navy top brass don't want to send everything they've got because that would mean pulling ships out of Norway and away from protecting the convoys. So we've got some destroyers and minesweepers down there, and they're OK getting people out of the harbour, providing the place doesn't get bombed to bits, but no good when it comes to the beaches, because they can't get in close enough. And the Navy hasn't got enough small boats to be any use. So far they've only got a few hundred people out. It's all going far too slow."

He paused for breath and took a gulp from the mug of tea Flo had given him. Wally looked thoughtful.

"So what you're saying is, expect a knock at the door to ask what *we're* going to do about it?"

"That's about it, Mr Read. If they can get themselves organized fast enough, they'll be talking to you and anyone else with a serviceable boat in the next twenty-four hours. Much longer than that, and it'll be too late!"

It didn't take twenty-four hours. It wasn't yet eight thirty on Monday evening when there was a banging on the front door of 38 Camden Square. Joe opened it. Wally was down the pub.

"Is your dad in?" a man with a domed forehead and a slightly shabby suit asked.

Joe told him where Wally was.

"Is it far then, this *Queen's Head*?"

Joe said it wasn't.

"Will you take me down there and introduce me, son?"

Wally was outside with some of the other boatmen, Bill Matthews among them. A pipe was clamped between Wally's teeth, and there was a half-finished pint beside him on a table. He was smoking the rum-soaked tobacco they called '*Pigtail Twist*', a boatman's favourite. Joe had tried secretly smoking some once and it had made him feel sick; Flo wouldn't have it in the house.

"I love my Wal," she said to her friend Elsie, "With my whole heart. I do. Everything about him. Except that dreadful pigtail stuff."

The man in the shabby suit cleared his throat to make himself heard over the chatter.

"Mr Read?" he said, "Sorry to disturb your evening, but we need a bit of help from you, if you're able to give it."

"Yeah, go on then!" said Wally, raising a knowing eyebrow towards Bill.

"We'd like you to stand by overnight with your boat for a job. All I can say at this stage is that it's a matter of vital national importance. If you've had your ear to the ground then you'll have an idea what it's all about. Now, how do you feel about that?"

Wally looked at Bill, who nodded, and together they grunted their agreement.

"The other thing is, I can't tell you exactly *when* we might need you," the man said. "So we'd like you to bunk down somewhere on the front where we can find you quickly. Would that be possible, do you think?"

"You could sling up some hammocks at Purdy's, if you wanted?" said Jim Anstey from where he leant against the pub door. Purdy's was the small funfair which remained obstinately and optimistically open beside the Pavilion.

Some of the local kids still went there with their pennies for a ride, but there'd scarcely been a visitor from outside town all month. And shortly the kids were going to be packed off to Stafford until things got better, so then there'd be no trade at all.

"Ta, Jim," said Wally, "Will yer throw in a few free rides? Might need something to keep us warm."

The man from the Admiralty stared at them all oddly. Were these men really going to be much use? They looked a pretty motley crew to him.

"Am I staying too?" asked Joe, when the Admiralty man had sloped off.

Wally looked at him doubtfully.

"Go on, Wal," said Bill. "He's a man now, give or take. And we might need 'im!"

"All right, then," said Wally grudgingly. "But run up and tell Flo what's happening first, Joe. Do you want 'im to get up to Bloomsbury Rd and tell Gert an' all, Bill?"

"Nah," said Bill. "Storm in a teacup, mate. Time enough when something actually happens. Believe it when I see it."

PART 2

DRAFTED

Tuesday 28 May 1940

It was a chilly night. Out beyond the canopy of the funfair, the stars twinkled brightly. The three of them tied their hammocks to the poles of one of the rides, but despite being inside a sleeping bag, and sheltered from the elements by the roof, Joe shivered his way towards dawn. It was bizarre to wake up and find himself among the brightly painted ponies, so strange that in fact it was hard to take seriously what might lie in wait for the *New Britannic* today.

"I 'ope no joker goes and starts this thing up," Wally had said before they went to sleep. "Otherwise we ain't half going to wake up quick! Be a bit rich, if we came to a sticky end on a fairground, before Jerry ever got 'old of us."

In the early light Joe heard Bill and his dad talking quietly.

"I keep thinking about Artie," whispered Bill. "And if, like, that's what we're going to do – pick up people and bring 'em home – wouldn't it be wonderful if it was 'im we found."

"Don't get your hopes up, mate," Wally answered.

"I'm just saying," Bill insisted. "It feels like it could be fate, or something…"

"Feels like a wasted night and a pain in the neck," said Wally, swinging himself out of his hammock.

The man from the Admiralty hadn't put in an appearance, and they mooched the few yards down to the harbour.

"Volunteers to shift mail off the *Sylvia*?" came a shout.

"Might as well, while we're waiting," said Bill.

Wally sniffed. "To think I was harbour pilot here once upon a time," he said, half-bitter and half-joking, "And now I'm just an ordinary scallywag."

When his dad had died, Wally had inherited the post of harbour pilot. But he'd never been well-suited. It was too respectable a thing. You couldn't go ducking and diving, and there'd been a bit of feeling among the harbour folk that Wally had too much of an eye on what was good for Wally rather than anyone else.

The boatmen had gradually been picking up more of the kind of casual labour the *Sylvia* was offering them. A few months back they'd have turned their noses up at the very idea, but these days anything which brought in the odd bit of cash was welcome. Better something than nothing. The *Sylvia* had been a regular visitor to Ramsgate for a few months since Dover harbour had become so crowded. She was rusty and ill-cared for, which was all to the good, so that she wouldn't be noticed as she quietly brought in mail from Calais and the more westerly French ports, keeping communications between Paris and London open. The shorter time she was in port, the better. That way the harbour was kept as clear as possible, and the *Sylvia* was quickly back at sea. Wally, Bill and Joe helped form part of a human chain, throwing the sacks across onto the harbourside, where a red Royal Mail van waited to carry the mail onwards.

When they were nearly done, Bill glanced back and saw the man with the domed forehead scanning the harbour front.

"Here we go," he said. "Our man's back."

They went and found him. Joe felt a stab of anticipation in his belly. Whatever it was that the *New Britannic* was to be asked to do, would Wally let him be part of it?

"Morning!" the man from the Admiralty greeted them. "Nice day for it."

"Depends what *it* is," said Wally dryly.

"As I said, we've got a special job for you. Where's your craft right now?"

Wally gestured to where the *Britannic* was moored, in mid-harbour.

"Good. Well, if you could bring her up to a harbourside mooring ASAP. And perhaps then go and have a word with Chief Petty Officer Adams. That's him over there? D'you see?"

A large truck with three Navy types had just arrived near the mail van. One of the men was waving his arms about – presumably C.P.O. Adams.

"The Chief Petty Officer will kit you out with some extra fuel, some food and a few other bits and pieces, and then if you can stand by, he'll get you moving soon after lunch. And now if you excuse me, I've got a few other chaps to see."

There was a little knot of men around them now, none of whom Joe recognized. Bill was talking with one of them.

"That's old Dudley from Broadstairs," Wally said. "Same business as us, more or less. And that's his boat out there – the *Princess Ida*. Dudley's all right, providing he doesn't sing at you. Goes for that hoity-toity Gilbert and Sullivan stuff. And I think the fellow next to him is a bloke called Benson from up Allhallows way. Goodness knows what he's doing here. I don't reckon he's ever been outside the Thames Estuary before. Search me about the others."

When they'd jostled the *Britannic* into a new mooring, the naval ratings handed them down cans of fuel.

"You won't be needing them for the time being," said the C.P.O. sternly. "And whatever you do, don't waste them. But I'm sure I don't need to tell you that. And when we've finished here, I suggest you go and sort out for yourselves as much drinking water as you can reasonably carry – you're going to need gallons of the stuff. Do you think you can find suitable containers?"

"No problem," said Wally.

"Gallons?" muttered Bill. "Shouldn't think I've drunk a gallon in me entire life!"

"Not for you," the C.P.O. said sharply. "There'll be a lot of people in and out of your boat. And a lot of them'll be wounded."

"Where are we going?" asked Joe innocently.

C.P.O. Adams looked hard at him.

"How old are you, son?"

"Eighteen," lied Joe, daring him to disagree.

"Well then, you're old enough to know I'm not going to tell you that. You'll find out soon enough. Right, I'm going to leave you in the hands of Supply Officer Moss. OK? But before I do, I need you to sign some papers. If you want paying for this shout, which I imagine you do, I'm afraid you're going to have to join the Navy for a month."

Wally pulled off his cap, and scratched his head as he looked at the papers. He didn't like it to be known that although his name was 'Read' – actually he couldn't.

"I don't know about that," he grunted. "What do you think, Bill?"

"Needs must, I suppose," said Bill dourly, scanning the few pages. He didn't fancy the idea either.

"Make sure it's only for the month, mate," Wally added dubiously, before he scratched his rough signature on the form. "Don't want to find we're press-ganged for the duration."

"And the lad…?" asked C.P.O. Adams. "Nah, don't bother about him…" said Wally, his mind working overtime, thinking about insurance and perjury and all sorts. "He'll work for free … if he comes at all."

Joe looked up and down the quay for Stan. He was bursting to tell him what was going on, but his friend was nowhere to be seen.

Moss helped them stock up the *Britannic* with blankets and food. There were tins of corned beef, biscuits and cocoa.

"There's enough here to feed an army," Wally said ironically, winking at Bill. Moss, who seemed to have no sense of humour, ignored the comment.

"You'll need some of these too," he said, pointing to the far side of the truck. A mixed bag of wooden and metal ladders had been slung there in an untidy pile. "Take maybe, I don't know, half a dozen or so, to suit the draught of your boat…"

Wally took off his cap, and scratched his head.

"Depends what for, don't it mate," he said, a bit stumped. "I'm having a bit of a job imagining… You mean for men to climb down into us, off a harbour? Or up out of the water?"

"Your guess is as good as mine, skipper…" was all they could get from Moss on that one.

But to keep him happy they selected a mixture and threw them all into the *Britannic*.

"Strip out everything except essentials, skipper," said Moss. "The masts can go. This won't be a trip round the bay.

And what about that bar affair in the bows?"

"It'll be a pain in the behind to take out," moaned Bill. "More trouble than it's worth."

They agreed the bar could stay in place.

C.P.O. Adams called a meeting for two o'clock.

"You'll be taken across the Channel under tow," he said. "That much I can tell you. And over the next hour or so, you'll see some of *Fervent's* complement of drifters begin to assemble at the harbour mouth. There'll be four of them, and here's how you'll pair up…"

The *New Britannic* was paired with the drifter *Northern Fortune*.

Wally looked askance at the thought of not making the trip under their own power.

"We don't need no tow-rope," he said grouchily. "Don't know about anyone else, but best leave the *Britannic* to make its own way…"

"Sorry skipper, I understand how you feel," Adams replied crisply, "But for all kinds of reasons, it's not on, I'm afraid. We swim together, or we sink together. We had a bad experience the other day on a similar kind of op. out of Dover, and lost a few boats. We don't want the same thing happening on this show. For the crossing, you'll be led by Commander Edwards from the tug *Holdfast*. Whatever he tells you to do, do it without question and at once please. Understood? The whole success of the mission depends on everyone working together. Any questions?"

"Joe," said Wally, "Just hop it up to Camden Square, and tell Flo we won't be back tonight. What about Gertie, Bill?"

"Not to worry. Flo can keep her filled in."

"You sure?"

"So am I coming with you?" Joe asked.

Wally genuinely still hadn't made up his mind.

"I don't think so, son…" he hummed and ha-ed. "What would yer mum have thought about it?"

It was a poignant moment. Wally so rarely talked about Daisy. Joe looked crestfallen. "You'll never manage with just the two of you," he argued back. "Suppose the weather gets bad."

"And what would I say to Nora, if you was to end up copping a Jerry bullet or drowned along with us?"

"Well then you wouldn't be there for her to complain at, would you?" Sunday's fear seemed to have vanished in Joe. All he could think of was being with his dad. He'd lost his mum. If he was going to lose his dad too, at that moment he felt he'd rather die with him.

"Look, just do as I've asked first, and I'll have made my mind up by the time you get back, won't I?" Wally grumbled. So Joe went as fast as he could, terrified the *New Britannic* might have left by the time he returned.

He needn't have worried. It was half past four before the signal to cast off came, and he'd been back at the quayside more than an hour by then.

"I've told Flo I'm going with you," he announced to Wally. "And she says quite right too. You need all the help you can get." What he'd actually said to Flo was, *Wally says he needs me with him. They won't cope without me.*

"He never did," said an astounded Flo. "What's the man thinking of, letting you go on such a dangerous trip. And putting the screws on you like that. I'll have words when I see him tomorrow. Just be careful, sweetheart. Give yer dad all my love. You're all such brave boys." And she enfolded him in a bosomy embrace.

What Joe didn't know, when he'd shut the front door on her, was that Flo cried her eyes out for the next hour or so, sure she was never going to see either of 'her boys' alive again.

A few yards from the doorstep, he'd passed a weary Stan Wainwright, who'd now slept just twelve hours out of the last seventy-two.

"Can't stop," Joe yelled almost triumphantly at Stan. "We're going in a few minutes… We're joining the Navy."

"What's this *'we're'*? Are you sure you should be doing this?" Stan asked dubiously.

"I want to be with my dad," he said. "It won't be any different in a couple of years when I'm out with him and Tom on the *Prudential*. There'll be plenty of danger then. Might as well get used to it now."

"Joe, this might not be quite like one of your usual lifeboat rescues," Stan said slowly, wondering how much to tell. "You know the *Mona's Isle*?"

Joe nodded. The *Mona's Isle* was a transport ship attached to *H.M.S. Fervent* and a regular visitor to Ramsgate harbour.

"Well, she only just about made it back into Dover on Monday evening, stuffed to the gunwhales with men. She got to Dunkirk OK, and pulled off more than a thousand blokes. But on the way back Jerry found her. They strafed her and hit her with shore-based guns. She limped back, and won't be going anywhere until they've done a massive re-fit. More importantly they lost twenty-three on the journey home, and at least another sixty wounded on top of the blokes who were already in pieces from being on the beaches. I don't want to frighten you, but that's the way it's going to be over there."

Joe gulped, and for a moment his stomach turned to water and his nerve failed. But how could he go back on what he'd said? He'd be letting his dad down, and almost as bad, he'd look a complete coward in front of Stan.

"I've got to go," he said. "Wish me luck…"

It reminded Stan of the time he'd watched his kid brother about to stick his fingers in an electric socket. He had time to shout a warning, but he could do nothing else. You couldn't live other people's lives for them, not even when they were family.

"Well, then you take care," said Stan reluctantly. He reached down to his belt and detached a small golden chain that was wound round it. "Keep him with you for a few days," he said. On the chain was a small St. Christopher, the patron saint of travellers. "Tell me all about it when you get back. You're a good man, Joe."

And he watched as the boy skipped round the square and disappeared into Albion Place.

At half past four, their little rag-tag convoy slowly assembled outside the harbour mouth, and began to head due east on a calm sea. Overhead the sky was cloudy, but the barometer was set fair. There'd be no weather problems for the next twenty-four hours at least. But was that good news, Joe wondered? On the one hand they'd have no difficulty seeing what they were doing. But then again, Jerry would have no difficulty seeing *them*, as the *Mona's Isle's* passengers and crew had recently found to their cost.

Up front was the Navy tug *Holdfast*, riding high in the water, reining in its powerful engines to allow the drifters to make whatever way they could with the craft they had in tow. It felt strange to the three of them on board the *New Britannic* to just sit there as the *Northern Fortune* pulled them forward at somewhere between a measly five and six knots. Joe didn't know the meaning of the word seasick, but the combination of the slight swell, and the lifelessness of the *Britannic* as she was dragged this way and that, made even him feel queasy. He occupied his time cleaning the engines, trying to make sure that when the moment came for them to be fired up, everything would be tickety-boo.

"Never knew what 'sitting duck' meant, till now," Bill shouted gloomily across at Wally from where he stood at the wheel.

"Make the most of it," Wally shouted back. "I don't get the feeling we're going to be sat on our backsides later on."

Some boatmen are good at doing nothing, and using spare moments to enjoy the chance of a rest. Wally had never been one of those. Any minutes not doing something (outside opening hours at *The Queen's Head*) was time wasted, as far as he was concerned. Now he paced up and down nervously, scanning the horizon for, well, whatever might be out there.

"Why are we heading east?" Joe asked.

Wally shrugged. "Well, it'll be one of two things, won't it!" he said wryly. "Or maybe three. Either it's about avoiding them minefields. Or it'll be to steer clear of the shore batteries. Or, they've been having us on, and the plan is, we're invading Germany!"

Their progress was painfully slow. It could only ever be as fast as the slowest of the drifters anyway, and at one point there was a pause for twenty minutes, while a couple of Navy grease monkeys tinkered with the stuttering engine of the vessel towing the *Princess Ida*.

Wally leaned over the side and watched as they scratched

their heads, before eventually resorting to belting the drifter's engine with a large spanner. He chortled and tutted. "Don't know their behinds from their elbows, do they, boy?" he growled at Joe. "You should get over there. You know a sight more than they do."

Eventually the drifter was reckoned to be repaired, and still they went east, as day wore on into evening, and the cloud began to lift and weaken. Behind them a soft grey and pink sunset slowly blossomed as the wind dropped to a murmur.

Bill shook his head. "We must be off Ostend by now. Where are these blokes taking us, Wal?"

But even as he spoke the words, the *Holdfast* began to sweep around to starboard, and set a south-westerly heading. The drifters followed suit like partygoers doing a conga, and as the sun disappeared and the night drew round them they made their way back towards the French coast.

This would have been a new experience for Joe anyway – to be this far from home in open water at night, even without the new and scary world that was opening up in front of them. Up until then, it had been hard to make out the sound of the guns because of the engine noise, but now, as their distance from the coast lessened, they could hear occasional violent discharges from heavy artillery, and more alarming still, the night sky occasionally lit up as a salvo found its target. Wally lit his pipe, and stared grimly ahead from the wheel. Bill kept watch. Joe hunkered down between the rows of seats with some blankets and tried in vain to get some shut-eye. And then, at about midnight, everything went ominously quiet for a while. Joe's imagination began to work overtime. He gave up trying to sleep, but as he looked out over the dark waters towards the shadowy grey-black boats up ahead, he began to think he could see a U-boat's sharky shape keeping pace with them. He imagined the captain watching them through its periscope, licking his lips with devilish delight as he chose the right moment to unleash death and destruction on the line of little boats from its torpedo tubes. Joe began to believe he saw the ghostly silhouettes of huge ships looming out of the inky blackness to tower above the *Britannic*, and more than once he was on the point of crying out to Wally and Bill, in case they were suddenly run down by a monstrous keel surging out of the dark. He began to shiver, and Bill looked towards him anxiously. "It'll be all right, lad," he said, although he himself wasn't sure it would be. "Steady as she goes. We've just got to hold our nerve."

Occasional patches of mist began to form, swirling around them, doubling their anxiety, firstly for what might be about to emerge from the mist, and secondly in case it caused them to lose contact with the convoy. And this was no ordinary mist. When it settled around them it had a burning, acrid quality, that made them want to cover their mouths, and search for a pocket of clean, clear air. They had their gas masks with them, and for ten minutes or so they fiddled around trying to fit them, till Wally swore, and threw his aside in frustration, unable to see well enough to steer. But despite the patchy visibility, the convoy somehow managed to stay together as the *Holdfast* changed its heading again to west-south-west. Then finally the tug gradually eased back on its engines even further, the convoy ground to a halt, and they dropped anchor somewhere around two thirty in the morning. Apparently they'd arrived – wherever it was they were supposed to be. With the engines of the tug and the drifters switched off or idling, they could now hear all around them a tapestry of noise: ships' engines, sirens, sporadic distant gunfire, although they could see next to nothing.

The three of them swapped very few words just then. There was nothing to say and it was the time of night when the brain insists on trying to shut down and find itself some peace. But at three thirty or thereabouts their uncomfortable and chilly dozing was shattered by a deafening explosion, and the night sky to the north-east was suddenly vividly illuminated by a sheet of flame. It dragged them onto their feet. Briefly they saw the outline of a British destroyer, maybe just two miles away. They watched in open-mouthed horror as in the space of no more than twenty seconds, the two halves of the ship peeled away from each other, turning and falling, crashing into the sea, and beginning to submerge, even as the water extinguished the flames, and the sea merged again with the blackness of the sky. Eerily, after the enormous force of the explosion, there was almost utter silence for a minute or two. Only a slightly stronger slap of wash against the side of the *Britannic* betrayed the fact that anything at all was wrong.

"God almighty," said Bill.

"What can we do?" shouted Joe, knowing full well the answer was absolutely nothing at all.

"What we're being paid to do," said Wally. "Sit tight, and pray."

Then they heard a crescendo of engines, and they gradually began to make out the wisps of searchlights playing on the water from a circle of ships around the scene of the disaster. In the eastern sky, the first signs of dawn were beginning to show. A rubber dinghy drew alongside the *Britannic*, and a voice shouted up to them from beneath a Navy cap, "You OK, skipper?"

Wally said that they were fine, and asked what the hell was going on.

"Torpedo attack. *H.M.S. Wakeful.* There may still be U-boat activity in the area, so please remain on station for the moment. Our orders are to move in at o-five hundred, whatever."

Wednesday 29 May 1940

It was perhaps a good thing that they had little time to dwell on what they'd seen. Joe knew that compared with the single death of the airman a few days back, what they'd just witnessed was something far, far greater in terms of human tragedy. It had to be possible that hundreds had died aboard the Wakeful, because the explosion had been so violent, and the ship had sunk so unbelievably fast. And yet it had all been like watching a film, somehow disconnected and beyond them. But although Joe had seen many films at the Picture House in Ramsgate, what he was to see next bore no relation to anything he'd ever experienced before.

As it became properly light, they started to take in the scene around them. They were maybe a mile and a half from a long sandy beach, backed with tussocky dunes, running roughly east to west. The yellow and green of sand and grass was covered with what at first sight looked like a speckling of driftwood, a flecking of brown and black, as if there'd been an incredible storm the previous night which had left the beach strewn with a year's worth of flotsam and jetsam. But on a second look Joe could see that there was movement in the rubbish, and he started to think it was more like the remains of an ants' nest which had been raked over, exposing and spreading the colony. But many of these flecks were human. Some were moving randomly, others with apparent common purpose. Other larger lumps of dark wreckage were really just that, discarded cars and trucks and guns, lying higgledy piggledy across the sand. To the west the pattern continued as far as the eye could see, which in fact wasn't that far, because a pall of smoke was drifting across from that direction, no more than five hundred feet above them, growing denser and darker the closer it came to where Joe presumed the town of Dunkirk must be. The smoke had spread well to the east of them too, merging with a grey sky as France turned into Belgium.

It was amazing to see the amount of traffic to the seaward side of them. A destroyer was already under full steam away from them towards the English coast, and they could see she was full to the brim with rescued men. Two minesweepers and a transport ship were in the process of arriving, standing off the beach, presumably making ready to receive passengers. A score of smaller boats were scurrying back and forwards between the beach and the larger boats. More sinisterly, there were the wrecks of at least three ships in view. Up to the east, an elderly paddle steamer lay marooned on a sand bar, and towards Dunkirk could be seen the remains of yet another destroyer and minesweeper, their backs broken. Joe thought how the death of ships was every bit as real as the death of people. These great beasts of the sea, once so vivid with life, were now just metal hulks, lumps of iron.

At a quarter to five, the dinghy was alongside again. The same weathered face as before was shouting up instructions to them.

"Still on track for o-five hundred, skipper? Very well then, we need you to power up and make for the beaches. There's not going to be a lot of ceremony about this, OK? Just find a suitable point where you're not in anyone else's way, and the men will come off the beach to find you. Don't ground yourselves, but let them wade out to you, understood? The beach shelves very gradually, so take it slowly first time in, till you've got the measure of things. Then when you've picked up a full load, your host ship is the minesweeper *H.M.S. Pangbourne*. Have you got that?"

Bill and Wally nodded.

"That's the *Pangbourne* over there, off your starboard bow. She'll deploy scrambling nets to take your men. Remember, slowly does it. Above all, don't overload yourselves. If you all end up in the drink you've become part of the problem. Work until eleven hundred hours, and then await further instructions. Good luck to all."

"Fire 'em up, Joe," said Wal. "Let's go and be good Boy Scouts."

The *Britannic's* engines purred into life, and at five a.m.

precisely, they cast off from the *Northern Fortune*, turned and headed for the beach. In less than ten minutes they were there, trying to find a space to do their job in amongst a tangle of motorboats and dinghies, who were all attempting the same thing.

A northerly breeze had been steadily rising over the last couple of hours, and although further out the increase in the swell was scarcely noticeable, closer in the wind was enough to whip up long folds of creamy surf. It was a holiday-maker's dream, but the last thing the *Britannic* needed. She pitched and yawed and the three of them were repeatedly drenched by spray as Joe slackened the throttle on the engines to bring her in towards the beach. They brought her about so that she faced the Channel and tried to hold a position in about five or six feet of water maybe seventy or eighty yards from the dry sand. Keeping the *Britannic* steady was almost impossible. With each breaking wave, all twenty-three tons of her was thrown vigorously from side to side, causing Joe to stagger and stumble as he tried to make ready with ladders and ropes. Already a line of men was wading out towards her. They'd watched the *Britannic*'s stuttering progress into the beach with longing, hungry eyes. Waving his arms, and shouting until he was red in the face, their captain had shepherded the soldiers into position to embark. Now they struggled through the water, some of them clearly at the limits of their strength, faces smeared with dirt under their tin hats, some holding a knapsack of treasured possessions above their heads. They'd walked fifty miles to reach this point, under fire and without much in the way of provisions, jettisoning equipment as they'd journeyed. Now just a few more painful yards and they were finally allowing themselves to believe they might be safe. Gasping for breath, and dragging their legs through the reluctant waters, they were scrambling to get a purchase on the sides of the *Britannic*.

"Let's try the ladders," shouted Wally to Bill and Joe, "But I don't reckon it'll do much good…"

And he was right. With the surf running as it was, the ladders were useless. There was no sure grip in the sand and with no secure attachment to the *Britannic*, they couldn't usefully support the soldiers as they tried to manoeuvre themselves aboard. There was nothing for it but to pull the men up by hand, one by one. Joe, Bill and Wally took turns – two on at any one time while the other manned the wheel. After embarking the first few men, Joe was already exhausted. His arms felt as if they were being ripped from their sockets.

"Take it easy, Joe," his dad shouted. "If we do ourselves in, this lot have got no chance."

Some of the able bodied coming aboard needed little assistance, but the wounded in particular needed to be pulled from above and pushed from behind by their mates. And inevitably, although most of the soldiers were just grateful to have got this far, there was occasionally the odd one who was panicking or desperate. Once a little gaggle of men tried to jump the queue, despite the insults their comrades hurled at them and the threats of the captain. Their assault on the side of the *Britannic* coincided with a particularly strong wave. The boat rocked violently and lurched in towards the sand. Bill seized a paddle, and swearing loudly, beat the soldiers away, yelling at them to wait their so-and-so turn. They told Bill exactly what they thought of him, but grumbling, eventually did as they were told.

It seemed to take an age to fill the boat, and still the men kept coming. For a trip round the Goodwins, the *Britannic* could take a hundred and twenty at a pinch, but there were more than that on board now.

"We can't take no more, Bill," Wally shouted. But the hands reached up pleadingly towards Joe, and it was hard to refuse them.

"Sorry mate," he said to the soldier right in front of him, who'd already taken a number of facefuls of surf, and who was fighting for breath in the cold water. "We'll be back in a mo. Just you hold on, now."

Slowly, weighed down by its heavy human cargo, the *Britannic* edged out through the surf, and back towards the waiting *Pangbourne*. As they pulled out through the shallows, Joe was horrified to see two dark human shapes floating in the water, arms extended, bodies bloated inside their khaki uniforms, faces ghostly white. They weren't the last dead soldiers he was to see in the hours that followed.

Wally took the wheel, while Bill and Joe lay with the Tommies up in the bows, almost as worn out as they were.

"This is the *New Britannic*, ain't it?" said one of them to Bill. He couldn't have been more than twenty, with a freckled face and sandy hair. His uniform was hanging off him, and there was a long, raw double cut running the length of his face from forehead to neck.

"How the blazes do you know that?" Bill answered.

"I'm a Ramsgate lad," the soldier answered. "I've been out to the Brake Lightship on the *Britannic* a couple of times when I was a kid. It was a good laugh."

"What's your name, son?"

"Matthews," the boy answered, "Ron Matthews—" Joe saw Bill start, and his face go white.

"The devil it is," Bill gulped. "My name's Matthews too – Bill!" he jerked his thumb back at the beach. "My little brother's over there an' all – Artie – with the East Kents. Don't suppose … you never came across him, did you?"

The lad shook his head. "Sorry mate," he said. "Not so's you'd mention…"

And Bill went very quiet. One man's good fortune used up another's, as far as Bill was concerned.

It took nearly half an hour to identify *Pangbourne* and draw alongside her. Joe was shocked to see that she was far from being fully seaworthy. It seemed she'd come under recent attack, and part of her superstructure was missing. There was bent and twisted metal everywhere. She didn't look entirely right in the water either, visibly listing to port. Scores of men were already hanging over her sides, and Joe guessed this was perhaps to be her last load before she struggled back across the Channel for repair. Those on the *Britannic* who could do so scrambled up into the minesweeper using the nets which hung down over her side, and those who were too injured to make the climb were winched slowly up onto her decks. There were some thank yous spoken to the *New Britannic's* crew, but most of the soldiers were too exhausted even for that.

"Cheers, mate," said Ron Matthews to Bill, "I owe you one. Maybe see you down the harbour sometime, when this lot's over?" From inside his little well of sadness about Artie, Bill somehow managed a weak smile.

Visibility had worsened by the time they made their second trip to the beach. The blanket of smoke from Dunkirk had fallen even lower across the seashore as the wind had died, and the day was turning out heavily overcast. Above the glowering clouds, they could hear the drone of aero engines, coming and going, circling above them. Their churning, grinding sounds set up a bubbling fear in Joe's stomach. He'd been brought up on the danger of the sea, in all its shapes and forms, but to feel his complete helplessness in this situation was something new, when death or injury could arrive from the sky any second without notice.

"Might be a blessing in disguise," said Bill, gesturing upwards at the smoke. "Whoever they are, they can't see us. Me, I like it that way."

The second trip was uneventful. The soldiers were orderly and well-commanded and the surf less strong. Because they were in water as shallow as Wally dared risk, the strain on their bodies was lessened because there was less heaving around of human flesh to do. Even so, Joe thought to himself that after only five hours work he was as physically exhausted as he'd ever been. He was bitterly cold, and soaked through, and the muscles in his legs and back were beginning to ache.

This time they were directed by loud-hailer to another minesweeper, *Halcyon*. While their passengers gratefully hauled themselves aboard, Wally produced bars of chocolate as the three of them slumped down, waiting for further orders.

"Where did you get those?" Joe asked.

Wally tapped his nose. "You just got to know the right people, son. Now drink some of that water, and get your head down while you've got the chance."

Almost miraculously, on the dot of eleven hundred, the tug *Holdfast* put in an appearance off their port side. The *Princess Ida* was keeping her company. In another five minutes a dinghy was alongside and the now familiar weather-beaten naval face was grinning over at them.

"Congratulations, *New Britannic!*" it shouted across to them. "Job well done so far. But we think we've got something for you and the *Ida* to do down at Dunkirk harbour. We'll pilot you over there to take a shufti. Stay close, and don't panic. Point is, the harbour's been shot to smithereens, and getting anything of any size in there's become a no-go. So frankly we're using you as a little test, to see what's achievable with something smaller. Thanks, skip."

"Well that's nice of them, ain't it," growled Wally. "*Little test*, my Aunt Fanny. Flippin' cannon fodder, if you ask me."

It took maybe nearly an hour to pick their way down the coast to the more easterly of the two long arms of the harbour walls which formed a flattened V-shape sheltering the port of Dunkirk. As the *Britannic* drew closer, Joe found himself entering a twilight world. With every minute, the sky grew darker. Behind the harbour, close to the town of Dunkirk itself, a dull angry red glow faded in and out of view behind billowing rolls of black and grey smoke. The harbour walls were hardly recognizable anymore. There were huge gaps in their surfaces, where the masonry had been blown away by repeated bombing, and even walking the length of them would have been impossible, let alone driving a lorry onto them. They followed the *Holdfast* to a point maybe three quarters of a mile from the jaws of the walls and to their east.

Bill summed up all their feelings. "Well that's a right mess, and no mistake," he said. "D'you fancy that, Wal?"

Wally shook his head.

Two destroyers lay at anchor, causing anything that wanted to enter the harbour to have to zig-zag between them. One flew the French flag and looked to be a critically injured ship, badly mauled by attack from the air. Its grimy and ancient British companion wasn't faring much better, but through glasses they could at least see its crew busying themselves on deck. Around and between the two ships a number of smaller craft motored aimlessly, but nothing was entering the harbour itself. As at the beaches, a line of ships could be seen out in the Channel, standing off-shore, hopeful of receiving evacuated men.

"Bunch of headless chickens," Wally sighed. He gestured at the darkened skies. "By God, it's as black as Newgate's knocker."

"What a hell-hole!" said Bill.

"Do you think we'll make it into the port?" asked Joe.

Wally turned his glasses onto the harbour walls.

"Well, there's not much sign of life up there. Wouldn't be much point, as far as I can see..."

The sound of fire from distant heavy guns had become so ordinary over the last hours, that Joe had largely stopped thinking about it. But now suddenly, ten seconds apart, there came two almighty whooshes that seemed to tear the sky apart with sounds like pieces of curtain material being ripped in two. Instinctively, all three of them dived for cover under the seats of the *Britannic* as two colossal explosions shook the harbour. Joe's ears rang. He was aware of his heart thumping against his chest, and then the shock waves rocked the *Britannic* from side to side. A siren began to wail somewhere in the town, and then a second one added its own sinister voice to the first. The distant gunfire continued, as before. They picked themselves up and looked over towards the harbour, but it was impossible to say where the shells had landed, or what damage had been done, if any.

"Oh, come on, what's the point?" said Bill angrily. "All that's going to happen here is we're going to end up brown bread, that's what!"

It seemed the Navy agreed with them. A few moments later a message came to them by loud hailer.

"Thank you, *New Britannic*," it said. "But no thanks. Harbour non-negotiable at this time. Please follow back to the eastern beaches to take on more trippers."

"Well, wasn't that a waste of bloody time!" said Wally. "Couldn't run a booze-up in a brewery!"

By three o'clock the *New Britannic* was back on station by the beaches off Bray, which they later learned was the name of the nearby village. They'd been without sleep now for more than twenty-four hours, and with each visit to the beaches, they were working more and more as if they were in a trance, each rescue mission blurring into the next. They spoke to each other and the men they were evacuating less and less. Their actions became automatic, to the point that Joe sometimes felt his mind and body had split apart. It seemed as if he was looking down on himself as he yet again stretched every sinew in his arms, legs and torso to drag weary soldiers into the safe haven of the boat.

Three more times that afternoon they went in to the beaches, pulling off a hundred and fifty at a time, and each time the confusion they encountered on the land seemed a little greater. The last time was the worst of all.

As they glided in, with the light just showing signs of fading, a fist fight seemed to be developing among the waiting troops. Even from fifty yards distance, Wally worked out why.

"Bloomin' Frogs! That's all we need!" he grunted.

Joe was so tired he didn't catch on at first.

"Frogs … Frenchies. Always wanting to be first." Wally continued.

"Never have trusted 'em … not since that day they kept us out of Calais!"

It hadn't dawned on Joe until then that there might be French soldiers looking for a safe passage too, but it figured. It was their country Jerry was invading after all, and their army was probably in as poor a state as the British one, cut off and facing imprisonment or massacre if they couldn't find a way to escape, just like the Tommies.

Down on the sand things were escalating rapidly. A British army officer was running forward, revolver in hand. He raised it skywards and fired a single time. The fighting soldiers turned to stare at him. He gestured at one group – Joe presumed it was the French – and waved them back towards the dunes. They stood their ground, spreading their arms and shouting abuse. One of them came forward and started to argue with the English officer, who again waved his gun threateningly and let off another single round into the air. But by then, the column of English soldiers had taken their chance and were splashing their way out to the *Britannic*. They boarded, still grumbling about what they'd do to any so-and-so Frog soldier who got in their way.

At eight thirty, the *New Britannic* was told it could go off watch until dawn. They were to expect to begin work again at 04.30. The *Holdfast* sent aboard some soup and bread for them.

"Try to rest up," the seaman who brought it to them said. "It's going to be another long day tomorrow. And the weather may not be on our side: the forecast's for clear skies, wind increasing Force 3 to 4. Sweet dreams to all."

Thursday 30 May 1940

Unsurprisingly, none of them got much sleep. The guns didn't let up all night, pounding away at the port, and judging by the backdrop of deeper rumblings, at more distant positions too. Jerry artillery, Bill thought – it could only be, by the staggering amount of abandoned equipment they'd seen littering the dunes at Bray. The Tommies couldn't have a lot left to shoot back with. Bill supposed that further out in the French countryside, the British and French forces must be vainly trying to hold off the German advance to buy time for the evacuation. Maybe out there somewhere, little Artie was holed up, hungry and desperate. Or maybe he was lying in a muddy trench, dead and uncared for, like so many thousands before him. Bill remembered the Great War of 1914–18, and realized how angry he felt. He didn't understand how things had come to this. How could the high and mighty politicians have fiddle-faddled around and allowed the best part of the British army to get trapped in such a way? Why had anyone ever trusted anything that evil little man Hitler had said? When Chamberlain had come back from Germany waving his scrap of paper, and saying 'Peace in our time', Bill hadn't believed it. So why had the British government?

Wally was having deep regrets. He even rolled over and said so to Joe, with a muttered "Sorry, son!", but Joe had dozed off and didn't hear him. He knew now he should never have brought the boy along. Wally was fatalistic about his own end – if your number was up, there was nothing you could do – and he'd been close to death often enough. He remembered the swinging boom which had nearly killed his own dad, leaving him unconscious most of a day, and befuddled for a week – the old man had never been quite the same afterwards – and he himself had carried corpses off wrecked ships a number of times. But how would he live with himself, if he came home all right, and Joe didn't? Joe's mum, Daisy, came back to him in his mind, scolding Wally for being so stubborn and thoughtless. For once in his life he prayed that if there was a God out there, He'd do an old sinner a favour and let them escape with their lives, heathen though they were. And then he cursed his own stupidity for thinking such a thing.

Joe slept better than the other two. To some extent he was just numbed by what they'd seen and done that day. As he drifted off he thought about Stan, and wondered what he'd say about the situation they now found themselves in. He wished he'd been able to show Stan around the tranquil town of Rye, and found it hard to believe that he'd been walking its quiet streets and feeding chickens at the smallholding only ten days ago. More than anything else he wanted the chance to go there again, and feel safe and protected, but right now, he couldn't believe he ever would.

They woke to blue skies, and a skittish breeze. Bill brewed up some tea on the Primus stove behind the bar, and they made a makeshift breakfast from some of the cans of food they'd loaded at Ramsgate. Joe found he had a sore head, and the rest of him ached too, but there was little time to think about any of that before they were back to work at the beaches.

With the new morning's improved visibility, the first air attack wasn't long in coming. They were just pushing back from the beach with their second load of the day, struggling to keep the boat on an even keel because of the uncertain wind and the sheer number of men clinging to the *New Britannic*, when two distant black dots on the horizon rapidly became larger. The dots followed the line of the beach from east to west, bearing in on them at great speed no more than a couple of hundred feet from the ground. There was barely time for a shouted warning or to glimpse the Luftwaffe insignia on wings and tail, before the planes opened up with an extended rat-a-tat-tat of machine gun fire, raking the beach with a deadly metal hail over a full mile or so. On the beach men dived for cover, into the dunes if they were near enough, or just throwing themselves flat on the ground, making themselves as small as possible, if the dunes were too far away. As the planes passed by, Joe was horrified to see that while some of those on the beach had been lucky, others hadn't. Dazed men pulled themselves to their feet to attend to wounded colleagues, calling anxiously for assistance or dragging the wounded back away from the dangerous seashore. Others stood over lifeless bodies, shaking their fists angrily at the sky, or betraying their helplessness with spread arms and drooping shoulders.

Joe had just taken the controls.

"For God's sake, get us out of here, Joe. Put your foot down. Jerry's going to be back any moment," Wally yelled at him. The line of the planes' attack, directly over the beach, had kept the *Britannic* safe, but common sense told Wally that if the pilots had their wits about them, they'd track out to sea a few hundred yards on their return pass, to try and catch a helpless boat or two. Eight knots felt painfully slow, as Joe, Bill and Wally willed the *Britannic* out towards the relative safety of the waiting ships. The Messerschmidts would be less likely to take on the Navy's anti-aircraft guns when strafing the beach was pretty much a risk-free activity. In fifteen minutes the *Britannic* was back in the shadow of *Halcyon*, and they were able to breathe a sight of relief.

"So where are our boys in blue?" Bill shouted. "Tell me, Wal, have you seen an RAF plane since we left Ramsgate? Do we actually *have* an air force, or are we just letting Jerry get on with it?"

113

In fact, later on in the day they did see several formations of RAF planes – Spitfires, Hurricanes and Defiants, but none of them stayed to protect the beaches. Mostly they flew on inland, or turned east at the coast towards the Belgian border.

"Well, to give 'em their due," said Wally grudgingly, "I suppose it makes sense to try and keep the Jerry planes away, rather than shoot 'em up here, when it's too late."

But if that was the plan, it didn't work. There were several more strafing attacks during the morning and early afternoon, and then towards lunchtime, on three occasions, Stuka dive bombers added their own voices of terror to the symphony of war. Stan had described their method to Joe back in Ramsgate, and now Joe was forced to see it for himself, and feel in his own stomach the gut-wrenching fear that this time the pilot had somehow from his bird's eye view personally selected them as his prey. They watched as the Stukas arrived noisily over the beach, and then, having pinpointed their targets, hurtled from the sky at a steep angle, using their direction of travel to aim their payloads. As they dived towards their unfortunate victims, they added a piercing scream from a siren to the sound of the engines, so that they frightened you senseless before they killed you. When it seemed the planes must crash, they pulled out of the dive, leaving the bombs to hold their direction, exploding violently on the ground. In the first two attacks the bombs seemed to land harmlessly in the dunes, throwing up clouds of sand, but causing no casualties. The third time was a different matter, and Joe looked away and put his hands over his ears rather than have to live forever with the pictures of carnage, the screams of the dying, the mutilated scraps of flesh that had once been soldiers.

They had their own encounter with a Stuka too. As they delivered yet another set of men to a waiting destroyer, and the able-bodied men were launching themselves at the scrambling nets with one last desperate reserve of energy, the destroyer suddenly threw its engines into 'Full Ahead' and lurched forward. A score of soldiers missed their hand and foot holds or bounced off the side of the ship, and swimmers and non-swimmers alike, were pitched into the sea, floundering around, gasping for breath. Joe was all for throwing himself in after them to pull out those who were struggling the most. Wally had to put restraining arms around his shoulders.

"Not now, son. Leave 'em. Let 'em work it out for themselves. We've got other things to do," he shouted, and then in the chaos, they understood why the destroyer had taken evasive action. A banshee wail from a Stuka siren was followed by a whooshing explosion off the destroyer's stern. The captain's brilliant manoeuvre had prevented an even greater disaster.

Despite the ever-present danger from the air, the number

of men milling around the beach never seemed to lessen. Each time the *New Britannic* drew in towards the sand there were more of them competing for passage to the waiting ships than the jumbled flotilla of rescuing boats could possibly cope with. Because of the squally wind, the difficulties with the surf and currents were even greater today, and the men on the beaches had begun to build makeshift piers for the boats to draw alongside, in the hope of making life easier. They'd driven lorries and cars into the sea, one behind the other, as many as fifteen a time. They'd shot out the tyres of the lorries and then filled them with sand so that once in position they wouldn't shift. Then they'd used anything they could find, wood or metal, to lash together a solid platform so that the men could scramble aboard without having to wade in the head-high water.

"Blow that for a lark," said Wally. "Nice try lads, but I think we'll keep going as we are. No point in bashing ourselves to bits on their piles of old junk."

"Quite right," said Bill. "None of it looks that solid to me. Could easily topple over and do for us all. Recipe for disaster, Wal. But you can't blame them."

How many trips backwards and forwards did they make that day? Eight? Ten? Twelve? Joe lost count, and one lot of war-weary, shell-shocked men merged into another. Only the most tragic cases left any impression on them. There was the boy who looked no more than Joe's age with half a leg shot away, slipping in and out of agonized consciousness in the arms of his mates. They tended his slight body the best they could, but it was clear the cause was hopeless. In the course of the short trip from the beaches to the waiting transport ship, he'd slipped from life to death. There was the man who'd lost his sight. His friends held his hands as he repeated pitifully, "I can't see owt, lads. I can't see owt..." There was the gunner who had more burned, seared flesh hanging off him than skin still intact, but who refused to show the least sign of pain. There were men so scarred that Joe wanted to turn his face away rather than look at them. In the face of so much suffering and need, Joe and the others worked themselves beyond the point of pain until their legs gave out, until all they could do was lie, utterly exhausted and almost delirious, in the bottom of the *New Britannic*.

It was about then that Joe looked out across the distance of the sparkling Channel waters and saw the sun glinting on what he at first thought was an unusually large flock of distant floating seabirds. Then as he watched from his dazed stupor he started to see the birds as a multitude of boats steadily making their way towards the French coast. There seemed to be hundreds of them, maybe thousands. For a few moments he didn't know whether what he saw was real or a mirage or whether he'd simply lost his mind. But the shot of adrenalin the extraordinary sight had given him forced him upright. Eventually he stood up and, pointing across the water, he said in an astounded voice, "Dad, Bill, take a butcher's at this!" It was no mirage. With every minute the miniature armada of boats was coming closer.

"Blimey," said Bill, "It's the cavalry! That's what that is. They must've rounded up every boat in the south of England."

There were yachts, wherries, cockle boats, fishing smacks and barges, excursion boats like the *New Britannic* and the *Princess Ida*, lifeboats, small motorboats that had never been downstream of London's Tower Bridge, tugs and ferries, you name it – if it floated and had some power, it was there. It lifted their hearts to see them. It wasn't that up until now they'd been doing the job alone – far from it – but the sheer number of boats and boatmen volunteering to put their lives at risk for the sake of the trapped soldiers was a sight to move anyone to tears.

"Flippin' Ada," said Wally, wiping his eyes with his sleeve. "What a sight!"

Legs turning to jelly, heads muzzy, eyes heavy, they stood and watched. In the first rank of boats approaching them was a familiar shape, flying the Royal National Lifeboat pennant.

"It's only the *Prudential*," shouted Joe. "Uncle Tom must be on board."

"Trust Primrose to get in on the action," muttered Wally, wanting even now to score points over the *Prudential*'s coxswain, but secretly proud that Ramsgate's own lifeboat was doing its bit. "Looking for a medal, I expect, like always."

The *New Britannic* had played its part now. As if by magic, the *Holdfast* again found them, and hooked them up with a drifter for the return journey to Ramsgate.

"You can stand down now, skipper," a disembodied voice shouted over to them. "Time for others to do the work. You can go home with the Navy and the nation's thanks."

There were no alarms during the crossing and Wally and Bill let Joe sleep like a baby until the drifter cast them loose outside the Ramsgate harbour wall in the early hours of the morning, leaving them to find – with some difficulty – somewhere to tie up inside.

"Did the *Princess Ida* sail back with us?" Joe asked groggily, still half asleep.

"The *Princess Ida* won't be going nowhere, mate," Wally answered grimly. "According to our friends in the Navy, she got herself shot up yesterday afternoon. No survivors, they reckon."

"Poor old Dudley. He was a good bloke," murmured Bill. "They'll miss 'im over in Broadstairs. They might need a new boat over there, Wal. What do you reckon?"

"I reckon whoever takes it on'll need to talk German. And that rules the both of us out." Wally replied.

Joe shivered, and not just because it was another unseasonably chilly May night.

Bill staggered home to Gert, while Wally and Joe held on to each other up the hill to Camden Square as if they were a couple of drunks. The key hadn't turned in the lock of Number 38's front door, before Flo was falling on them, bawling her eyes out, and covering Wally and Joe with hugs and kisses. Wally fended her off.

"I never thought you'd come back," she blubbed. "I was sure those murdering Jerries would shoot you or blow you up. I don't really believe it's you here, now."

"Make us a cup of tea, will you love?" said Wally. "I'm gasping."

Friday 31 May and Saturday 1 June 1940

Joe slept fourteen hours straight from the small hours until late Friday afternoon, and even then in Flo's opinion he wasn't fit to be allowed out, and on this occasion, in her house, she had her way, although she let Wally drift down to *The Queen's Head* for a mid-evening pint. Joe didn't understand why he felt the urge to cry all the time – although he'd never do that in front of Flo. He so badly wanted to stop replaying the events of the last seventy-two hours in his head, but however hard he tried to think of nicer things – of Rye, and getting up to mischief with Stan, and of sunny days with the trippers around the Goodwins, all that he could see in his mind's eye were decayed bodies floating in the water, men drowning when seconds before they believed their hands had touched safety, soldiers torn apart by the violence of high explosives.

"Where's Stan?" he'd asked Flo when he woke up.

"He had to work tonight. Sent his best wishes, and hoped he'd catch up with you tomorrow morning," she answered. "I've not seen him myself for more than five minutes since you've been gone."

"There's still thousands of blokes out there in France," Joe said to her, suddenly restless, stirring from his chair. "I shouldn't be sitting here. We ought to be going back to bring them home. Where's Dad?"

"Don't talk daft," she said. "You've done your bit. More than your bit. Wal should never have taken you in the first place if you ask me, and he knows it. So now just let it go, will you?"

And in fact, Joe really didn't have the physical or mental strength to argue.

The next morning, he still felt groggy, and unusually for him, he hung around the house for a good part of the day, listening to the radio, reading the paper, unable to settle to anything, as if he was convalescing from an illness. Despite his promise, Stan failed to show up. The Navy was a hard task-master, and he was probably stuck at his desk up at *Fervent*. Wally had gone off early to fix up the *New Britannic*. By the time they'd returned on Friday morning it was looking bloodied and battle-scarred.

In the late afternoon, boredom finally made Joe get up and go out to find his dad, but by then Wally and Bill had had enough of cleaning, sanding and varnishing, and had retired to sit outside the pub, waiting for the doors to open.

Joe walked along the harbour front, letting a lovely summer's day make him feel more human. A number of people said hello, and waved greetings. Word had got round about the *New Britannic's* exploits. The front was a different place to usual. Hundreds of troops in various states of repair were arriving, pouring off boats of every shape and size. Their clothes were often in tatters, and some scarcely seemed to be wearing any clothes at all. They looked haggard and gaunt. Young faces seemed to have gained lines you'd have expected to see in men twenty years their senior. As the heroes arrived, the people of Ramsgate welcomed them with open arms, pouring coffee and tea down parched throats, throwing towels and blankets around their shoulders, offering supporting arms as they made their first teetering steps on dry land, and escorting them to the buses which ferried them up to the station for their onward journey. Except most of these men didn't feel the least like heroes. They felt like failures – an army in retreat, having sacrificed comrades, equipment, and the land they'd been meant to protect. Amongst them were many French soldiers, doubly confused and depressed. They wandered around like lost souls. They spoke no English, and because very few Ramsgate folk could speak any French, no one knew quite what to do with them.

Strolling among the crowds was Alderman Kempe. He caught sight of Joe and greeted him like a long-lost friend.

"Master Read," he cried, crushing Joe's hand in a vice-like grip. "Well done, young man. You're a credit to your family and to Britain. I've been hearing all about your exploits, and

I have to say all Ramsgate should be proud of you."

Joe muttered a thank you.

"Is your father well? If he hadn't taken the *New Britannic*, I daresay he'd have been first in line to be on the *Prudential*. I hear she's doing splendid work on the beaches too."

Joe said that his dad was fine.

"I've been in touch with my friend Miss Marchant. You met her last week, remember? She's promised to write an article about the work of our Ramsgate people in the evacuation. I imagine you'll be mentioned in dispatches."

Joe looked doubtful. When so many had been killed and injured, it didn't seem right to talk about what the *New Britannic* had done. And he wondered if Hilde Marchant's article could get Wally and him into trouble, because after all, he'd been underage, hadn't he?

How precisely Alderman Kempe read Joe's thoughts it was hard to say, but seeing Joe's face, he added, "Well, maybe no names, no pack drill. The important thing is that we British are standing together in the face of tyranny. Always have. Always will. Now give my regards to your father when you see him, and tell him I look forward to thanking him for his bravery in person soon."

There was a bit of to-do at *The Queen's Head* when Joe got back there. The pub had only been open a few minutes, but the first pint had been swiftly downed, and Bill and Wally had probably had a rum or too beforehand. So it was exactly the wrong moment for a bunch of loud RAF lads to swan in from Manston in their smart little MG sports car, laughing and joking, and demanding quicker than quick service. It got Bill Matthews' goat, and he was letting them know it.

"Why don't you get back to work, and do what you're supposed to be doing, instead of drinking yourself silly?" he shouted at them. There was a mutter of support from some of the bystanders. "La-di-da fancy boys leaving our lads for dead on the beaches, and grandstanding around the town instead of being real men and killing the Hun... I don't know how you live with yourselves."

The drink had made Bill emotional. He felt sure Artie was never coming back, and he was grieving for his lost brother. The normal Bill would never have started on anyone like that.

"Now just hang on a mo," said a posh-sounding young airman. "I reckon we're every bit as much real men as a bunch of common, drunken layabouts. What have you ever done for King and Country, old man?"

And that did it. For a moment, it looked as if a major fight would take place, until Wally dragged Bill away, and the wiser heads among the RAF contingent restrained their idiots. But the atmosphere on that part of the harbour front didn't recover for the rest of the evening. A thunderstorm was threatening: it was hot and oppressive.

"How many do you think we saved, Wal?" asked Bill

tipsily. "What do you reckon Joe?"

"I dunno," said Wally. "More than a thousand, however you look at it."

"A thousand?" shouted Bill, "More like three…"

"Nah," Wally replied. "Never that many. Think about it. How many trips? And how many blokes a time?"

Bill fell back into silence for a while, and then, about five minutes later added, "Well you could have filled a football ground with 'em. That I do know."

Sunday 2 June 1940

Joe and Stan walked up towards Ramsgate's railway station on Sunday morning to watch the evacuees leave town. Everyone said it was a real sight up there. Stan couldn't get over how quiet Joe was. It worried him.

"Are you all right, then?" he asked for about the third time, looking across anxiously at the younger lad.

"Yeah, I told you," Joe answered.

"What was it like, then? It must have been unbelievably scary."

"Nothing to tell…"

"Really?"

"I don't want to talk about it, OK?"

And they fell back into silence again.

While he'd been sweating away in the *New Britannic* all Joe had been thinking was how he'd tell his story to Stan if he ever got back, and how impressed Stan would be. Now the moment had come, he didn't know where to begin. There was a tightness across his chest, as he held back the fear, pain and exhaustion, and he was worried that if he said the slightest thing, it would end up in unmanly tears. Maybe, if he'd seen Stan the day after they'd returned, he'd have been able to talk, but not now.

After a while, when they were almost at the station drive, Stan said, rather too brightly, "Well, I've some news, anyway."

"What's that?" Joe asked, glad to be able to talk about something else.

"I'm being posted."

Joe was completely dismayed. All he could think was how unfair life was, that on top of everything else, having just found a best mate, he was about to lose him again.

"I only heard yesterday. They're sending me off to sea," Stan added.

"But I thought you said you was a hopeless sailor..."

"Well, ships need fuelling and feeding. And you have to go where the Navy tells you. It's a promotion, a reward for doing so well at *Fervent*, I suppose. Maybe I should have messed up a bit more…"

"When do you go?"

"I have to report at Portsmouth on Friday for the destroyer *Wild Swan*. She's being re-fitted there. You probably saw her during your French trip last week. She copped a couple of shells, and they're sorting her out now."

"Where will they send her, when she's finished?"

"How would I know? The top brass play their cards close to their chest. If you asked me to guess, I'd say the west coast of France. There's going to be action down there in the next few weeks, that's for sure. They won't want the French navy falling into German hands."

"I'm sorry..." Joe managed.

"*You're* sorry. I'm frightened out of my tiny mind..."

The scene at the station was extraordinary. Joe and Stan couldn't get near the platforms at all. It seemed as if the whole of Ramsgate was leaving town. It would have been chaotic enough if it had only been the army. Sorry-looking groups of evacuated soldiers in an assortment of badly-fitting clothes were being waved this way and that towards waiting trains, or being held back for future dispatch. No one seemed to be listening to anyone else, and as many soldiers were re-emerging from inside the station in confusion as were being sent there in the first place.

And then there were the children. Before the rescue from Dunkirk had ever been dreamt of, this Sunday was the day that had been selected to evacuate Ramsgate's schools from the town. Crocodiles of tearful children lined up with their teachers, clutching suitcases, gas masks and teddy bears. Watching them were as many grieving parents waving handkerchiefs, making feeble jokes and trying against all the odds to be brave for the sake of their little sons and daughters.

"Too many goodbyes," said Stan turning away. "I can't cope with this."

"You'll keep in touch, won't you?" asked Joe in a small voice.

"I'll do my very best," Stan answered. "And if it gets difficult wherever the *Wild Swan* ends up you know I'll be thinking about what you three did going off to France with the *New Britannic* this last week."

"I think you ought to have this back," said Joe. And he unwound the St. Christopher from around his neck, and put it in Stan's hand.

"Knock, knock," said Stan, fingering the good-luck charm.

"Who's there?

"U-boat."

"U-boat who?"

Stan made a pretend moustache across his top lip, and in a bad German accent said, "U-boat must come with me at once. Do you understand?"

Joe couldn't help but laugh.

September 1941

The *Daily Mirror*'s car collected Joe from Camden Square at half past eight.

"Chauffeur-driven," cackled Flo, calling up the stairs. "Just like a film-star. See how famous you are. You won't want to know us after this. Now let's see what you look like..."

Joe flinched as she brushed his collar and straightened his tie.

Wally was off somewhere up the Thames with the *New Britannic*. "Load of nonsense," was all he'd said about it.

The journey to Hailsham took a couple of hours, and the driver wouldn't stop talking.

"So what's this all about then?" he asked, when he'd given Joe his opinions about Churchill, Hitler, Stalin and why didn't the flippin' Yanks get off their lazy backsides and do something useful. "How come I'm driving you all over Sussex?"

Joe squirmed around on the car's front seat. He was nervous, and his nerves made him talk, for once.

"Well, last year me and my dad got involved in the Dunkirk rescue in our boat, the *New Britannic*. Then it got into the papers, but they didn't say our names or anything, just that I was only fifteen when it happened. And then these nippers in Hailsham started trying to find out who I was, and they wrote to the mayors of all the towns along the coast, and eventually they wrote to Alderman Kempe – he's the mayor of Ramsgate – and he said he knew who I was. So now they want me to go and meet the kids at the school."

"Good for you, mate," said the driver. "We need a few stories like that to cheer us up!"

At the school, they treated Joe like royalty. They sat him down in the headteacher Mrs Upton's office and gave him tea and home-made fairy cakes. Then he was introduced to the *Daily Mirror*'s reporter and photographer and after a few minutes Mrs Upton led them into the school hall which was packed with children sitting cross-legged on the floor. In front of the children a long trail of pennies stretched the width of the hall.

"Now children," said Mrs Upton, "We have a very special guest with us this morning, one you've been longing to meet all summer. This is Mr Joe Read, who helped rescue thousands of men from the Dunkirk beaches. And remember children, when he did such a brave and wonderful thing, he was only a very few years older than the top class in this school. Now Mr Read, the children have spent their time collecting these pennies by helping with the harvest, doing housework for their mothers and blackberrying. In all they've collected five pounds, which Samarra is now going to present to you with a card they made themselves."

A girl shyly came forward and gave Joe an envelope. Neither of them was quite sure what to do, but the photographer organized them into a smiling handshake.

"It could have been our brothers you saved," she said. "And this is to recognize and thank you for your courage."

"And now perhaps you'd like to say a few words to the children, Mr Read?" the headteacher asked.

Joe had been dreading the moment. He took a deep breath, and in a faltering voice he said, "It was nothing. Anybody would have done what we did. I was used to taking our little boat around the lightship on pleasure trips for the holidaymakers, so I knew all about handling her. My dad and I just did what we could."

THE END

133

Historical Note

The Read Family

Three years after the Dunkirk evacuation, Joe was called up into the army. Wally kicked up a fuss about that, and with the help of Mr Balfour the local Member of Parliament, Joe eventually saw service as a merchant seaman on a Scottish ferry which had been converted into a hospital ship, the *Duke of Argyll*. Later Joe worked on tankers as part of the convoys which brought Britain the vital supplies needed to win the war.

After the war Joe came back to Ramsgate. He married a local woman, Edith Spain, who already had a little boy called Graham. He set up his own business as a fisherman while continuing to help his dad out during the summers with the *New Britannic*. He was a member of the Ramsgate lifeboat's crew from time to time too, alongside his father and uncle, and was involved in at least one famous rescue. By 1954 the *Prudential* had come to the end of its useful life, and the new Ramsgate boat, the *Michael and Lily Davis*, was called out with others to the South Goodwin Lightvessel which had broken adrift in terrible conditions. So bad were the seas, that despite desperate efforts, no one could get near enough to her to prevent disaster. In the end all the men on board the Lightvessel drowned, except one. The survivor was a young birdwatcher from the Ministry of Agriculture and Fisheries.

As he got older, Joe became very unwell with cancer, which limited the amount he could work and go to sea. He died in 1981, at the young age of fifty-seven.

From time to time various people have re-discovered the story of Joe, Wally and the *New Britannic*. In particular, there seems to have been a BBC television feature in 1965 to celebrate the 25th anniversary of Dunkirk, and some fine still photographs of Joe, Wally and their boat date from then. Perhaps unsurprisingly, Joe was reluctant to talk about what he'd seen and done, even to his stepson Graham, and the occasional interviews he gave to newspapers don't tell us much. At the best of times he seems to have been a man of few words, a doer rather than a talker. But you have to ask yourself what the effect was on the rest of his life of those few terrible days in 1940. Did he ever really recover?

Many civilians put their lives at risk during the Dunkirk evacuation, but as far as anyone knows Joe was the youngest. Perhaps the fact that there were so many who answered the call is the reason why so few received official recognition. As sometimes happens, the better known you were beforehand, the more likely you were to be noticed. Howard Primrose Knight, the coxswain of the *Prudential*, deservedly received a

Distinguished Service Medal, and even Joe's uncle Tom was given a special certificate of thanks from the RNLI along with the rest of the *Prudential's* crew. Joe and Wally got …nothing. The *Prudential* was away from home for forty hours, the *New Britannic* for nearer sixty. In terms of the number of men rescued, both boats are claimed to have helped in the low thousands, although it's hard to be sure about that.

During the rest of the war the *New Britannic* became a Royal Navy tender, supplying ships around the Medway river. Then afterwards, she returned to working as a pleasure craft in Ramsgate. When Wally finally retired in the mid nineteen-sixties, she was bought by Albert Mastin who kept her going for a few more years. He eventually sold her on too, and after a spell in Weymouth, she found herself in the Scilly Isles, specially equipped to take disabled passengers. In recent years the *New Britannic*, temporarily renamed the *Commodore,* has had a chequered history, and spent some time sunk at her moorings in Falmouth harbour. However now she's back at Ramsgate, where she belongs, being restored for a second time under her original name.

Because Joe and Wally were essentially very private people, it's not always been easy to find out the details of their day to day lives. In the dedication at the front of this book you'll see the names of some of their relatives, still alive today, who've been very generous in telling what they know and remember. The Maritime Museum in Ramsgate has also been an invaluable source of information.

In Part 1 of this story, some of what you'll have read is a writer's imagination trying to re-create life in early wartime Ramsgate. For Part 2, there are a few more of Joe and Wally's own words to draw from, and of course there are many other historical accounts of the valiant efforts of the 'little ships' to rescue the British and French forces. But so that you know the major things which are true and those that have been made up, here's a short list:

Camden Square:
Still exists in part, just to the east of the centre of Ramsgate, and is where the Read family probably owned a number of houses. The area was bombed and shelled by the Germans quite extensively in 1941. Some Read family members were injured at that time.

H.M.S. Fervent:
Was indeed based in the Merrie England Amusement Park, which was itself built around a disused railway station.

Stan Wainwright:
Stan never existed, although there were many naval ratings like him working in Ramsgate.

The Ramsgate caves and shelters:

The work described as being done by Alderman Kempe and his Borough Engineer to protect the residents of Ramsgate is historically accurate, and a bit of research on the web will lead you to pictures of the old air-raid shelters as they are today. And there are certainly workings in the chalk dating back to earlier centuries which were probably used by smugglers, though not in the precise location I've described them.

The weekend trip to Rye:

The Sussex town of Rye was an important place to young Joe for the reasons described.

John Le Mesurier:

Was a real-life actor, most famous for his role as Sergeant Wilson in the TV series *Dad's Army*. He was a frequent visitor to Ramsgate and along with other celebrities was known to the Read family, although possibly not as early as this.

Alderman Kempe's day out:

The only time the *New Britannic* was ever used for any fishing activity was once a year for the Mayor and his friends, but this particular trip is an invention.

Hilde Marchant:

Hilde was a distinguished journalist who wrote for a number of national publications. She's perhaps now best known for her description of the lives of women and children during the London Blitz. She was one of those who wrote about Joe, in her case, in the *Daily Express* newspaper.

Archbishop Cosmo Lang:

Archbishop Lang was the local bishop, as well as being head of the Church of England, so he knew Ramsgate well, and was entertained by Mr Kempe more than once – but just not on the occasion described in this book! And the Duke of Kent also paid visits to Ramsgate, notably once in 1939 to see the air-raid shelters.

The Royal Navy ships present at Dunkirk:

Those mentioned were involved in the Dunkirk rescue at some point, but it's impossible to say whether Joe and Wally would have worked with them. The *Wakeful* was attacked and sunk in the way described, but although from their own accounts it seems the Reads saw a British warship destroyed, we can't be certain it was the *Wakeful*.

Arthur Matthews:
Bill Matthew's little brother Arthur never returned from France. When the details of the casualties were finally announced, Bill and Gertie learned that Artie had died somewhere on the beaches during the evacuation.

The trip to Hailsham:
Is more or less as described in a *Daily Mirror* article of autumn 1941.

Dunkirk and the war:
What happened during those days in 1940 is often called a miracle. People have sometimes put the 'miracle' down to the way in which the nation observed the Day of Prayer on 26 May 1940.

On the other hand, whatever you think about that, maybe the evacuation from Dunkirk – Operation Dynamo – was a miracle which shouldn't have been necessary. The political and military leaders in Britain were slow to react to a situation they should have seen coming. They badly misjudged the ability of the French to defend their own territory.

It's sometimes fun to play the *'What if?'* game when studying history. The *'What ifs?'* of Operation Dynamo are alarming. If the British Expeditionary Force had been wiped out or captured on the beaches of France (and most British politicians including Churchill feared that it would be), then Britain would have been largely defenceless from invasion. The knowledge that our army had been destroyed surely would have encouraged Hitler to go for all-out victory. And if Britain had been subdued, all of Western Europe would perhaps have ended up permanently in Nazi hands.

The United States of America wasn't yet in the war, and there were a lot of Americans who thought it should stay neutral – that this should remain a European problem. For the time being they would probably have made peace with Germany, although how long that could have been maintained, it's hard to say. German agents were already active in South America.

Germany would have always struggled to overcome Russia, but the reason it eventually failed to do so was partly the need to fight on two fronts simultaneously. If Britain had been added to the Nazi resources, maybe Stalin's Russia also would have fallen.

Getting our troops back home was the first step towards the eventual defeat of Hitler's Germany, even if it seemed a mixture of disgrace and relief at the time. But as Wellington said in another context, it was a 'damned close-run thing'. Firstly the weather was very kind to the rescuing boats. For days the waters remained relatively calm. If the seas had been more awkward, far fewer men would have been taken off the beaches and out of Dunkirk harbour. Secondly

Hitler acted cautiously in moving to finish off the exhausted British troops. His armies had brushed aside French, Belgian and Dutch resistance in not much more than a fortnight. It had been a dazzling military success, and now he was caught in two minds between seizing the prize of Paris, and eliminating the British army. To be fair, he had concerns about the tiredness of his own men, and communications were sometimes difficult along his long battle lines. But he hesitated at the wrong moment, and he also failed to allow Goering's Luftwaffe the freedom they wanted to go on all-out attack against the Allied armies caught in the narrow strip of land along the French coast.

Hitler's hesitation gave the British just – and only just – enough time to organize the rescue. This was Winston Churchill's first great moment during the war. He had only been made Prime Minister on 10 May 1940, the day our story begins, and although many people didn't like or approve of him, somehow he was able to assert enough authority to get the job done.

Even more difficult times were ahead. Six weeks after Operation Dynamo, the Battle of Britain began in the skies over southern England, and by early September, London was coming under daily bombing in what became known as the Blitz. But thanks to Joe and Wally Read and hundreds of others like them, that summer Britain at least had a fighting chance of holding off the German threat.